I Da

The Saturday Challenge
*Bundle of All 6 Novellas in
The Sex Challenge Series,
A Day of Play*
Ruan Willow

Table of Contents

Dedication

This book is dedicated to lovers who play in and out of the bedroom, those who never stop playing, and those who desire to please their partners and get off on getting their partner off, plus celebrate who they truly are because that's how it should be. Openness in sexuality should be celebrated and is a blessing.
Try new stuff! Fulfill your fantasies!
Mutual pleasure is mutual bliss.
This book is erotic romance, please read and enjoy it knowing this is the genre it is in.
Marinate in your sexuality daily.
"When I told you I'd love you forever, I had no idea it would be this easy."

Book 1:
The Kitchen Sex Challenge

The rolling pin clunks to the floor, narrowly missing my right foot. Damn lucky. That would have hurt. I wiggle my toes, the silver of my toe rings glistening beneath the blaring kitchen track lighting, the little fake jewels that I love stealing the most shine. One of my favorite gifts from my bachelorette party last month. Smiling, I recall Lana handing me the little gift bag, which also contained a sex toy, not the usual gift from a daughter to a mom, especially for a second marriage. But she gets it. Her beautiful blue eyes were all a twinkle as she placed the gift in my hands. That was more of a gift than anything that day.

And honestly, that had helped ease the pain a bit. Every day the pain of leaving him had haunted, but that had ultimately been squashed by the agony that would have come from staying. It wasn't that George had been overtly abusive; it had been the million and one small things he did to manipulate. His ever-present reach for perfectionism had been what had made me a prisoner. Death by toothpicks, spiked ones that sneakily held tiny shards that, over time, made giant gashes. Little comments of disapproval and rampant, pervasive disappointment can choke a woman to near death after twenty years.

A shudder runs through my body as I hug myself. Being single at forty-four wasn't what I had expected of my life.

But meeting Brad had changed all that.

My smile peaks at the thought of him, yet it's a bit wistful as I swipe the flour specks off my feet, littering the dark wood floor beneath in white specks. Stubborn flour. I rub harder to clear my now white speckled red toenails, as if the snow-filled sky had blown into our kitchen. I glance outside and Maxi is jumping in the fresh snow like she's living popcorn, taking bites of snow the same way she attacks a treat. The backyard is one big snack to her.

I glance towards the staircase. Ugh. Still no sign of Brad yet. Maybe I need to go upstairs and just grab him by the cock and drag him down here by his morning wood. I giggle. He'd most likely love that. Something my ex would have abhorred because it was out of routine.

I grab my phone and check for a text from Brad. Nothing there either. He needs another naughty pic.

I shake my head. "Up way too late for work last night, my love," I mutter to the empty kitchen. Though I know even if he didn't sleep, he'd come down those stairs with a smile. Something that I value more and more each day.

I blow up the picture I sent him an hour ago via text. My boob hanging out the side of my apron, nipple in full bloom erectness, complete with my areola bumps announcing themselves, my hand on the curve of my hip showing off my recent manicure, my lips in a generous pucker. I had my thigh raised, partially lifting the apron over my groin. He must still be asleep to not have responded to that pic. I snap a picture of the bareness between my legs and send it to him.

"That all oughta bring him down here quick when he finally opens those peepers up," I mutter to myself.

Back to work now. These cookies won't make themselves. Hell no. In fact, if it weren't for the tradition, I'd skip it, being it's now January and the holidays are over. They are such a pain in the ass to make. So meticulous and painstaking, having to cut each damn square, load it, and fold in every other point tries my patience every Christmas season. But I gotta make these cookies, too much of a tradition to skip, even this year with the craziness of the wedding at holiday time and all. And, really, too damn tasty to not make. Tradition is tradition, even if it happens in January. I know somewhere Grandma is smiling.

I lean down to pick up the rolling pin, pissed that now I need to wash it again. Something fatter than a finger slips between my butt cheeks and I jump up, squeal, and drop the rolling pin again. It clunks loudly on the hardwood floor once more.

"Oh!" I whip around and immediately notice the little pink rubber whale-looking kind of thing in Brad's hands. His handsome face is set in the largest grin possible. "Oh damn. You scared me. What is that?" I give him a sly grin.

"Good morning, Anna, the love of my life. It's a toy. A new one. For you. For me. For us." He pulls me into his arms, his dark full lips in a full grin in the middle of his graying goatee. His eyes twinkle as his mouth swells into that sexy smile I can't ever resist.

"It looks like a whale. Bath toy?" I grin, biting my lip as he presses his boner to my belly. "Been waiting for you to wake up. Did you see my pictures?"

"Yes. Gave my morning wood a boner." He leans down and plants a kiss on my forehead, his lips lingering so long I can almost feel the ridges. He plants a kiss on my closed lips. "This could be a bath toy. That's a plan for another day, though." He sighs and lets out a slow whistle. "You look beautiful in this apron."

He nuzzles his face into my neck so swiftly I let out a squeal.

"Whew. A double boner, that's hot." I run my hands down his biceps, savoring the softness of the flannel against his hard muscles beneath, a gift I gave him when we had just started dating a year ago. Aunt Trish always said, the older you are, the faster you marry. She was right. "I still love these pajamas on you. My sexy lumberjack."

He slides his hand down my naked side, the little pink toy flops against my bare hip as he sways me back and forth, cradling me in his other strong arm. He tucks my head expertly under his chin.

I take a deliberate breath in. He smells like him and mint, with a splash of fresh cologne.

"Well, I certainly have wood for you." He chuckles huskily. "Sorry, couldn't resist that one. You said something related to wood."

I want nothing more than his wood, but I smile, and a giggle slips out. "Cheesy. Real cheesy, Romeo."

He drops his jaw in mock surprise. "Hey, I thought you liked cheese."

I give him my bedroom eyes. "Just saying." I bite my lip. "But. You know. That little whale looks kind of like a sperm."

"Sperm whale," he says with amusement. A flicker of lust flares in his eyes as he twitches his cock against my belly. "Nice apron, by the way. Did I mention you look sexy in it?" He nibbles along my neck, down to the mounds of my breasts.

I moan and snuggle into his arms. "You already said that. And hardy har har har. Hilarious. Don't all whales make sperm? All mammals fuck. Why do they get the notoriety?" I reach down and give his right butt cheek a squeeze, which prompts him to slap my ass with a naughty grin stealing over his face. "You are oozing the cheese out today."

"You touch mine, I touch yours." He raises an eyebrow at me, then shows me the gleam off his super white teeth.

"Promise?" I go up on my tippy toes and he obeys, leaning down, and a full-blown pucker smashes my lips. I lower myself so my feet are flush on the cool wood floor again. "I'll hold you to it forever."

The click click click of the living room clock seems louder than normal as I catch my breath, wishing I could just chuck the dough in the fridge and pounce on him for a round of quick kitchen sex.

He takes my face between his hands, the smell of the linen soap from our shower wafting off his still dewy skin. "You'd better."

He takes my lower lip into his mouth and sucks it, rubbing it with his tongue before entering my mouth for a deeper kiss.

I might just melt into air. How did I get this lucky to find this man while browsing for cookbooks in the bookstore? That day he had been shopping for a rare Wisconsin hot dish cookbook, some old but once mega-popular book he wanted to surprise his mom with. She was eighty-five then and still loved to make big hot dishes, saving portions as frozen dinners to shove into her already full freezer, some of which I enjoyed more than I ever cared to admit. All of those mini-meals now sadly occupy our freezer space. That day he had a black trench coat on with expensive-looking shoes peeking out from his dress slacks. The gleam in his eyes suggested he knew how to fuck a woman into several orgasms and then oblivion. That look, and the diligence with which he carefully examined each cookbook until he found the right one, sold me over before he even opened his mouth to ask me out for a cocktail. I'd have to have been a blind asexual fool to not pounce on such a lusciously lust-filled man.

I pant against his chest, more and more wanton for him by the second.

He pulls back from our kiss, leaving me craving even more to shove him to the floor and ride that boner he's pressing into my gut into twenty orgasms or more, screaming like a banshee in heat the whole time. His intense stare wrecks my resolve every damn time.

"What are you making?" And his smile could melt the freckles off my cheeks If I'm not careful. He leans down and licks my right nipple, which had slipped out the side of the apron as he jostled me.

My hands fly to my cheeks as they heat with pleasure. A little squeal penetrates my lips. "Um." What was I supposed to be doing again? Fuck. He makes my concentration bottom out. Oh yeah, he asked me a question. I close my eyes so I can answer without looking at him. "Oh. Yeah. I'm making

Christmas tarts." Refocusing on my task, I reopen my eyes. "They are an old classic cookie recipe my grandma used to make. After she died, I picked up the tradition."

"I don't remember those last year. Did you make them?" He nuzzles his goatee into my neck, his mouth savoring my skin in a slow suck and kiss. He's the kind of man who would remember that.

I'm turning to floppy putty in his hands as he mouths me.

He gives a little satisfied grunt, though unmistakable and delicious.

I moan, writhe in his arms, my head falling back. If he doesn't stop, I'm going to fall into a wild tryst with him and this dough is going to dry out, be ruined. I glance at the beige mound of dough, seriously half tempted to say screw it and let him make love to me right here in the kitchen, and just start a new batch tomorrow. Or maybe if I wrap it really tight in plastic it will last until tomorrow. "I did make them last year. I must not have shared this kind with you. I do save a lot for my dad and aunts since I'm the only one left who makes them now."

He pouts, the twinkle never leaving his eyes. "I need cookies too." He releases me and dips his hand in the flour bowl. He spins me around and bends me over, placing his flour-coated hand on my naked buttock. "Your butt looked like it needed a handprint."

I giggle and squirm away from him. "Oh stop!" I shiver like I just stepped into a cold shower. "I hope that hand was clean, or you just contaminated a whole bowl of flour."

He claps the flour off his hands.

I resist the urge to grab a tissue to wipe the flour from my ass. "So, tell me about this toy. Is it on the agenda today?" I'm so hoping he has another one of his famous sexual plans cooked up. He thrills me with his sexual ingenuity, and I'm not intimidated by his advanced sexual experience, at least not anymore. I've learned to let him pamper me. It was a huge challenge at first to let go, to let him be in charge of my body, but it's so massively rewarding, not to mention scrumptious.

"Oh, yes. I'm going to play with you all day long." He holds up the toy and grabs his cell phone from the counter. "See, this toy is going in your pussy. Then I'm going to tease, shake, tingle, blast, and vibrate your sexy pussy so much that you will forget these cookies and beg me to fuck you."

I raise an eyebrow at him, the slow realization of what he's proposing settling in. A slow burn grin travels across my face in a smirk. "Oh really? Is this a challenge then?" I let the full sparkle of this tease play out as I let it fully reach my eyes.

Mischief skitters across his face and settles in the wrinkled corners of his smile. "Bat those hazel beauties at me, sweetheart. If it's a wager you want, I'm in." His nod tells me he's serious, and he's going to win.

"Okay. Name it." I tear off a hunk of dough and set the rest aside. Flattening it, I remind myself I still need to wash that rolling pin. It's probably now covered in dog fur from the floor.

"Hmmmm. This has got to be good." He taps his forefinger to his nose, his thumb tucked under his chin. He strokes his goatee as his eyes tell me he's cooking up an expert-level plan in that fabulously sexy brain of his.

I run the rolling pin under the water and slop dish soap on it, rubbing it quickly with my hand to soap it up instead of grabbing a washrag. I can feel his eyes burning into my bare ass as I dry off the rolling pin. Glancing back at him over my shoulder, I ask, "Enjoying the view?"

Him tapping his finger to his temple reminds me I need to go see if Maxi is at the door, which also reminds me I need to buy more dog food and schedule her vet appointment. What the hell? Rabbit hole. Why am I thinking about all that? I glance out the window before I leave the sink. Maxi is still hopping about and chomping mouthfuls of snow like it's food.

"Oh yes, I am. Loving my claiming of that ass as an actual visual."

I shake my ass at him.

He moans, watching me as I roll out the hunk of dough. "I will bet you a twenty-minute massage, where the giver is naked too, that I can make you come with this toy and beg me to fuck you ... before you get all of these cookies done."

I guffaw, flare my eyes wide at him. "Whoa. That's not fair. These take forever to make. They are so meticulous and intricate. I'm at a serious disadvantage here." I throw my hands in the air. "They are really a slow go, which is why no one else makes them but me." I wield my knife in the air. "I have to make four cuts on each dough square at the corners, fill each of the tarts, and fold in every other point to make it look like a star." I sigh for effect. Blow a puff of wind upwards to make my hair flop. "Then bake them, not too long, not too short, just until the tips start to barely brown. Then take them out quick." I roll my eyes. "It will take me hours."

"Good. Then it's a fair game to test your resolve." He grins as he snags a piece of dough and pops it in his mouth. "Mmm. Yum."

I scoff. "Fair? Seriously?" I raise my eyebrows as I shake my head. "I don't know about this." I drag my finger down his handsome jawline. "Oh, you are a doughboy, huh?"

As I roll the dough flat, my big breasts wiggle. My right one slips free when I roll hard to flatten the dough to proper thickness, the way mom taught me years ago. I glance up at him, his facial expression appreciative. I'm getting more turned on by the second, with him rubbing his lower lip with his tongue.

"I'm pretty sure I could watch you do that all day long and never get tired of it. You know I was kidding last night when I said I wanted to see you cook dinner naked, but now I'm super glad I said it." He raises his eyebrows at me multiple times. "Because look at you now." He lets out a low whistle.

Butterflies erupt in my gut. It's like I'm fourteen again, and the cute boy has taken an interest in me.

"I liked the idea, so I thought I'd surprise you." I grab my knife and raise it, ready to start cutting. "My grandma taught me when I was seven. It was always her way, me making these cookies with her every Christmas." The day was always a busy one as we made six different kinds of cookies, all double batches. My mom had always got stuck wrapping the bazillion caramels Grandma cooked up, which had to meticulously be heated to the perfect temperature, leaving my sisters and aunts to do the peanut blossoms, my cousins to do the cutouts, and my dad to unwrap all the chocolates. We called ourselves lucky if he didn't eat too many.

The glow of that memory heats up my insides. This man brings such priceless goodness to my life. Every day he makes me smile.

I eye him up and down, taking in all his rugged handsomeness. An idea trickles through my brain. Oh, my man, I'm getting in on the scheming this time.

"Let's sweeten this challenge. Whoever begs the other for sex first has to fulfill the other's unfulfilled fantasy. A long-awaited one." I flash him my naughty grin.

The pearly sheen of his teeth a brilliant contrast to dark hairs in his goatee as he mutters, "Oh, I'm so in."

"Your kids stopping in today? If so, I guess I should give up the naked baker theme. It's often their way to just pop in, you know." And dare I say I love it. Our families have blended together so effortlessly, even more nicely than I ever hoped possible.

He grabs a coffee cup from the cupboard and sets it in the Keurig. "Nope, not that I know of. They usually text, though, so I would be forewarned. Usually," he says skeptically. "I'm pretty sure Kailey has to work today so they won't come, I bet."

"Mine aren't coming either. They're busy. I'm just glad they bothered to call me to even tell me." The thoughts of them both going off to college still leaves a lump in my throat each time I let my brain revisit that memory. I miss them so much. It's hard to not have your babies living with you anymore. But I couldn't be prouder of who they've become.

He wiggles the pink whale-looking sex toy in the air, the lower part clearly heavier as it swings like a pendulum. "Anna, you ready for me to insert this? I'm pretty much drooling out the precum hoping to start up this bad boy asap."

"I think I'm at a disadvantage in our wager here. I will be manually stimulated, and I'm thinking it is going to make me cave first, and it's a given you will win. We need something to edge you."

He chuckles, his eyes alit with a secret. "What you are wearing does that all by itself, honey. I'm a man. Remember, we are all visual imbeciles. Show us a mostly naked woman and our brains lose power to our dicks." He chuckles haughtily again. "Consider me already edged to the max just looking at you in nothing but that apron. I want to bend you over this counter and hard fuck your brains out right now."

His dirty talk and conviction send a twitch through my clit. He's a generous lover that pervades every layer of our relationship. I bite my lip to hide my growing lust. And good, he's way more than half-cocked already. I give him a sultry, flirty look. I try to calm my breathing as that familiar luscious lurch curls inside my gut. It dances inside me when he expresses how much he wants me. It's like magic. I take a step back from him, like his lust is physically sparking out at me.

"That one gotcha, didn't it? I can tell." His grin tells me he knows, and that he loves it more than life itself.

I try to hide my smirk. "Well ... " I suck my lip into my mouth and a small guffaw slips out of my lips, betraying me. "Maybe." Yeah, I can't hide shit from him. He reads me like a damn kid's storybook, easy as pie.

"Ain't no maybe about it. I just made your clit twitch, didn't I?" he gloats like he just landed the best deal ever.

Oh. How does he know me so well? And how is he so damn irresistible? I set my face in a blank expression, as best I can, and drop a spoon into the apple filling. I'm failing miserably.

He pokes my side and wiggles his finger.

I stifle a giggle and squirm away from him.

He grabs for me and pulls me close. Tucking my head against his chest, he releases a slow moan. "Let's get this party started, babe." He taps the sex toy on my back. "Wanna fuck?"

"So. Not. Fair," I mutter.

"What? You can say whatever you want to seduce me too, ya know."

I nuzzle my face into his chest and nod. I can't stop the laugh that percolates out of my smiling lips. "I'm ready. Let's do this." I lean back and gaze into his kind eyes that switch to an ever-growing mischievousness right before me.

"I'm horny as fuck and I have a devil on my shoulder this morning." He pulls open the utility drawer and grabs our kitchen lube.

I smirk. "Clearly so." Who the hell has kitchen lube? We do. We are kitchen fuckers. Who am I kidding? We are whole house and backyard fuckers.

He releases me and squirts a splat of lube onto the sex toy. He swiftly smears it all over the large bulb of the toy.

"That thing looks interesting. I imagine that tail whipping my clit."

He laughs, his chuckle reaching his eyes in full blast. "Nope, it's not quite like that. Trust me. You will love this, though. I will love this. We will love this." He gazes directly into my eyes. "Okay, spread your legs, babe. I'm going to tease, tickle, titillate your clit. Get ready. I'm going to push you to your limits. Make you moan and scream out with pleasure." He clears his throat. "As many times as I can today."

I lift my right leg, gripping my thigh just above my knee as I brace myself on the counter with my other hand.

He caresses my labia lips with the toy, petting me.

A moan flies out of my lips. "Mmmmmm. Yes. Oh." Wishing all morning for him to touch me has me in overdrive. I'm in big trouble.

He tickles his fingers along my labia lips and sneaks his fingers inside. "So wet already, sweetheart."

"Yeah." I sigh as I lean back against the counter, my head dropping back. I bite the corner of my lower lip as I release a soft sigh.

The edges of his lips raise as he wiggles his big thumb into my cleft, presses it firmly against my clit.

I groan out and tip my head back even more, gasping, gripping the marble counter. It's completely unsatisfying. I need to dig my fingers into something, so I dig my nails into my thigh and jerk with a wince.

He places the tip of the toy to my pussy entrance and rides it up and down along me, pulling out and spreading my wetness along my skin. He firmly grabs my chin so our gazes lock as he wiggles it against me. Our connected stare is seductive as fuck, so much so I'm ready to shove him to the floor and rip his clothes off. He's known how to woo me from the start of our whirlwind relationship.

His deepening smile melts me as he gently inserts the toy into me. His grin drifts into that sexy, naughty grin of his that he saves for such moments as this.

I'd most certainly give him anything, even that which I fear giving.

I let yet another moan fly out as he pushes the toy fully into me. My nipples harden as I gasp, my heart pounding away like a machine gun. The toy slides in me so smoothly. "That feels amazing already," I mutter softly.

"Wait until I make it move." He nestles the little tail along my clit and my lower lips fall around it, securing it in place. "There we go. Tuck this guy in right." He presses the toy up to nestle it in place inside me.

I reach for him, unable to resist touching his cheek. I run my fingers down across his goatee and rub my fingers across his lips. How wonderful those lips felt across my breasts last night. I never knew such sexual heights before I met him.

He kisses my fingers, then takes them into his mouth for a suck.

As I lower my leg, he grabs my shin to stop me.

"Wait, one more adjustment."

Kneeling down, he tips his head so his lips line up with my groin. He gives my sensitive skin a kiss, followed by a tongue swipe along the toy. He wiggles his tongue the length of the tail, tantalizing my swelling clitoris.

I moan out and tangle my fingers into his hair. I press his head snugly into my sweet spot. I'm so in big, big trouble. He's totally going to win. I've already practically lost. I moan again, reveling in how amazingly he treats me. I never question my importance in his life. Ever.

He presses the little button on the end of the tail. I hear a buzz as it vibrates once inside me. He glances up at me, then holds up his phone and points to it.

"Now it's time for me to play." He sticks his tongue out to run it along his top lip. "Carry on with the cookie-making, babe. I'm just going to take my coffee and my phone to the living room and watch the show." He holds his phone up again and he shakes it, barely hiding his giant lecherous smirk. "Can't wait to see your reactions. You know how I love to pleasure you. To see you react. Study you." His crotch is sporting a massive erection.

I scoff. "Oh, I'm the show." I pretend to be offended. My lips curve into a snarl, but I let my eyes tell him I absolutely love his teasing.

"Best show on Earth, babe. Best show on Earth. Nothing else I'd rather watch than your body reacting to pleasure. Especially pleasure I'm responsible for." He raises an eyebrow. "You, my beautiful wife for life, are going to lose."

"Oh, is that so?" I say with snark before I wrinkle my nose and give him my most intense bedroom eyes.

"Whew. With that look ... " He snags a strawberry-filled croissant from the tray, and a napkin as he leaves the kitchen, headed for our plush couch, no doubt.

I stare at the dough, wondering about my next move here, his next move. I cut the dough into squares while I keep glancing at him settling into the living room, wondering when he will send me the first twitch.

He's fluffing pillows, setting up his food and coffee on the coffee table, switches on a lamp, turns on the fireplace. When he picks up his book rather than pushing buttons on his phone to turn the toy on, I almost cry out. Fucker is doing this on purpose!

He glances my way, and his eyes are in full-on flirt mode. He coughs. I jump.

I'm ready to burst. "You are just teasing me on purpose, aren't you?" I yell across the house. I throw my arms in the air and do my best to give him an exasperated look. Though I know I'm too far away to be effective.

He chuckles.

"He's such a punk-ass," I mutter under my breath.

"What's that, my love?"

Okay. I'm going to ignore him. He's enjoying this way too much already. Not that I blame him one little bit. I focus on my dough squares. Tarts, yes, I'm making these tarts. I cut two slits where I should have only done one. Fuck. I can't concentrate worth shit. I try to fix it, but they end up uneven in size.

"Fuck," I mutter. Now they won't cook evenly, so I scrunch up the last one and add it to the big dough ball. I release a sigh of frustration.

The toy inside me begins vibrating with a low hum. It's pleasant, not overstimulating by any means. I don't even jump as it gently massages my insides. My grin grows as a slow burn across my face as I cut a slit along each of the corners of each dough square. Dare I say, it even helps me focus, not scream my head off. I keep my face stoic as I scoop up an apple from the can and plop it in the middle of the first dough square.

The toy starts to vibrate harder and faster inside me. My breath catches. I lurch forward with a gasp, dropping the spoon to the counter. Its clang reverberates in the otherwise silent room. I moan despite all my efforts to not.

I swallow my lust enough to say, "It feels really nice, by the way." I glance his way, wondering if he noticed my sounds.

He points my way and gives me a nod before taking a big bite of his strawberry croissant. "Good. That's what I like to hear." He chortles like a little boy who was just given a chocolate bar. "And I know. Gonna push you beyond a vanilla 'nice' though."

I bite back my smile and release a sigh to try to refocus my brain on my task. I scoop out another apple and position it over the next dough square when he gives the toy inside me a huge surge. My arm flails in response as I let out a squeal and my upper body instinctively curls toward the counter. The apple falls on the cutting board with a juicy splat, nowhere near the middle of the dough square. "Oh, fuck me!" I yell. Holy shit. Holy shit. I'm screwed. He will win. I know it.

He returns the vibration of the toy back to the calm, nurturing mode. "You alright in there, babe? Just gave you a little twitch." He snickers like a bully.

I glare at him. Oh well shit. That was little? I'm totally screwed. He will certainly win this challenge and I will have to fulfill his biggest unfilled fantasy, which could actually be a fun thing, but I'm dying to know what he would pick. Plus, I just want to win.

I shoot him a polite, nonchalant look. I grit my teeth as he sends some little burst to the toy. I set my jaw firmly. I'm totally winning this challenge. I attempt to throttle back my heavy breathing.

"Oh, I'm great, my love. Just great," I manage to say without letting out a moan.

I scoop up the misplaced apple and plop it onto a dough square. He's going to ride me hard and strong. All day. I eye up the big ball of dough. It's huge. It's going to take me hours. There is literally no way on this infamous Earth that I will last longer than this massive dough ball. Not with these slow meticulous tarts, which are entirely way too intricate to make for how quickly people eat them. Blasted tradition! I'm doomed.

"I'm just over here making Christmas cookies. In January. I'm just as perfect as can be."

I'm not admitting defeat already. I suck in a breath slowly through my parted lips. But, in all truth, I love nothing more than giving in to him. I'm his and he knows it. All my joy in that. I lick my chapped lips, vowing to dig for lip balm before I roll out another dough ball.

He gets up and saunters to the Christmas tree. He fixes an ornament. And another one, probably things he doesn't really need to do. Then he straightens the ribbon. He's just trying to fake me out. "We should take this down soon, huh? Being that Christmas is long over."

I watch him without moving my head as I scramble for a lip balm in the drawer. I used to have five little tubs in here. "What the fuck?" I mutter as he sends me another burst through the toy. I smear the balm all across my lips, doing my best to ignore the sensations flooding my body from my pussy.

"Right, babe?"

I nod. Wait, what are we talking about?

"Getting those lips ready for my engorged friend, are you?" His cajoling tone is making me want to smile and pout at the same time.

Dammit! I'm looking at him and not making cookies. I'm slowing myself down. Focus. I flare my eyes wide at the dough, realizing how fully mean this all really is. I begin the folding in of every other point of the dough, then securing it by pinching all the points together hard at the center. Now they look like pretty four-armed stars.

He asks Alexa to play Christmas music. How did I miss not turning on Christmas music this morning? I mean, I'm making Christmas cookies for fucks sake. That's usually the first thing I do. Too horny to think straight, I guess. Fuck, I'm a mess.

"Christmas in January," I mutter lightheartedly.

Maxi barks at the door. Perhaps her tummy is finally full of snow. I shuffle over, walking like a stiff. I slide the door open to let her in. An arctic blast of frigid air follows her inside the house. I shiver from the cold just as he sends the toy a jolt. His giggle is like a little boys' again, yet totally salacious. I lurch forward and try hard not to grin, but I lose. He sends a series of bursts and I suppress a scream as I sneak a peek at him. Yep. He's smiling damn big.

Maxi's completely covered in snow. Little snowballs decorate her limbs, dangling like so many little ornament balls. They jiggle as she walks.

"Well, aren't you full of snow, Maxi sweets? You better go lay by the fire so you can melt." I lean down to pet her, brush some snow off, and he sends a huge surge to the toy. I almost fall with a gasp. "Oh, fuck me."

I don't dare look at him. I don't need to. I know the expression he's sporting.

He hoots a whistle and Maxi bounds toward him, all her snowballs bouncing violently as she jogs. "You all right?" he asks, the question laced with teasing.

"Oh, I'm good alright. Perfect in fact. It feels good. It's a good toy."

He sends several bursts in succession. "Well, the word good is what you use to describe your neighbor's new hairdo. Not what you use to describe a sex toy rocking your clit."

"Hmpf," I huff.

Yeah, it feels way too good for me to win. I gently pick up and place each tart on the cookie sheet, ensuring each little dough arm lays flat and doesn't curl, or it won't cook evenly. I smile remembering my Grandma having to fix each cookie I placed down, and she never once scolded me, her smile a permanent expression the entire cookie-making day. She just wanted to spend time with everyone, to keep our traditions alive, to create memories. She had told me once before she died, don't worry about the things in life. Worry about the who's of your life. I always imagined the Who's of the Dr. Seuss books when she said that. The little Who's, those microscopic creatures that lived life so big on such a tiny flower. Little things don't know they're little, and that they are surrounded by bigger things they can't see, they live their best lives with joy. Grandma's wisdom can't be beat.

"What should we have for dinner tonight, babe?" He pets Maxi and picks more snowballs off of her and drops them to the carpet.

I scowl. I don't like wet socks. I glance down at my bare feet. Though they are already getting flour coated, I don't want them wet too.

I lift my eyes to my dough. He sends a long stretch of strong pulses. I gasp, jerk, and squeeze the dough ball between both hands, making huge finger indents, like little caves. It helps me not yell out to scrunch it between my fingers. I can't even speak for a moment before I burst out. "I don't care. Anything." Panting, I try to slow my breathing down, unable to stop my grin from taking over my face.

He looks as if he's forgotten what we were talking about as he laughs heartily from the couch, looking all relaxed and regal with his feet propped up in slippers, his chin jutting up into the air. "Feeling something over there, are you, babe?"

"As you sit there like a king?" My hands fly to my mouth to try and block my smile.

"I see that smile, babe. You can't fool me." He jerks his head back as he clears his throat. "I haven't even begun to tease you yet, my sweet little pussy willow."

The day he started calling me pussy willow was the day I caved, a day I'll never regret, even though we'd only been dating for a few weeks. The branches in the half-emptied trees above us shook in the light breeze, a rare warmish day in October, yet warm enough to have sex holding onto a tree trunk. My clit had twitched as he worked my capris down, my pussy had already soaked the fabric from all the dirty talk he filled my ears with on our walk. The lust that screamed out from each of his movements as he pushed me up to grip that tree had left me breathless. But still, I had to stop him for just one second so I could set down the lovely fragile branch from the pussy willow tree. I had snapped it off the bush when he was on the phone ten minutes prior, near the big rock where he first kissed me, and stole my heart for good. He had stopped the press of himself into me long enough to chuckle as I set down the little branch on the log next to the tree he was going to fuck me against. Calling me the sweetest pea, then pussy willow, he then proceeded to pound me so hard and primal that I was launched into the most epic orgasm of my entire life. I knew. This fucker was marriage material and he already downed me like a cheap chair, he could pick me up and carry me anywhere and I'd form to his body just so he'd make me feel like that again and again.

"I see that smile growing even deeper, baby. What are you thinking about right now?" He stands and approaches the kitchen, phone held out in front of him, fingers poised ready to tap out the tease of my pussy into another tizzy.

"Oh," I said, the dough smooshing in my hands as I pressed the ball flatter. "Nothing."

"Don't give me that, pussy willow. What is it? I love the look on your face right now, so I'd love to know what's bringing it there to your beautiful face, making you even more beautiful, by the way." He wastes no time and comes right up to me, caressing my arm with his full hand.

The bulge in his pajama bottoms makes all the female places in me water.

When our gazes meet, his eyes tell me he gleefully just caught me ogling his crotch.

"Fess up."

"Okay, it was when you first called me pussy willow. And I just knew I'd let you do anything you wanted to me, and that I'd love it."

He crosses his arms over his wide firm chest. "Ah yes. The famous first fuck. I knew you'd be in my bed forever after you let me pound you against that tree. Damn. That was such a good fuck, wasn't it? We need to do that again." He pauses as a look of lust invades his face. "And, anything?"

I scoff. "In summer, yeah. Right now, no thanks. I don't think snow-fucking is on my bucket list."

He shakes his head. "What if we were in a sleeping bag, a double-wide?" His eyes beam like he's ready to pound me into oblivion.

"Oh, damn. Now I've given you an idea, haven't I?" The little toy in my pussy is not feeling so little right now as it shatters my resolve with too many pulses to count. I glance at him, suppressing a guffaw. "How are you doing that? Your hand isn't even on the phone?"

"Oh, isn't it?" He grins as he pulls his hands to the front of him. He slides his finger around on the screen in a circle and it makes the toy inside me crescendo and dip with varying levels of vibrations. I try hard not to react, but my body betrays me as I jerk with each strong pulse.

"Whew. Holy shit. That's insane," I whisper after he drags his finger down.

"Yeah, when I take my finger off, it stays at the same mode, so I can do things like take a sip of coffee or pull snowballs off Maxi while still stimulating your pussy. I can multitask." His face is set in such amusement, I could never dash it.

I scoff, which ends in an uncontrolled snigger. "Wow, I didn't think you had it in you to multitask."

He flares his eyes at me. "Oh, cheap shots, huh. Remember, I'm the one controlling your pussy, my pussy willow."

"Why do you think I said it?" I smile, biting my tongue as it slips out of my mouth a bit. I dance as he drags his finger up to the top of the screen and I screech out. "Oh, my Gawd! Holy fuck!" I grip the edges of the extended cutting board in front of me, pressing down too hard, making it bend slightly. I fear I may crack the wood.

I pant as he slides his finger back down.

"Nice," he says followed by a light belly laugh. "It's kind of like playing with a remote-control car."

Somewhere in me something boils, pushing me dangerously closer to that climax edge. I release my grip on the wood of the cutting board. I pant, my voice coming out in puffs. "Boys and their toys." I shake my head. I grip the rolling pin hard. "Just don't make me drop this rolling pin on my toes, okay, lover?" I raise an eyebrow at him and give him a smirk.

"Oh, I'll wait. And I believe this is your toy, not mine." The look of jesting on his face is preciously randy.

"I beg to differ," I say with the fullest intent of haughtiness I can muster.

He glances back at me as he walks out of the kitchen, his eyes alight with mischief. "Okay, it's our toy."

I roll out the dough flat as I can, resisting the urge to just watch him and see when his hand flies up, so I will have notice for what's coming. But then, maybe that's cheating. I roll and roll until the dough is thin enough. With the toy on low, I make perfect cuts in the dough, the right length and angle in towards the middle.

The stereo belts out "Jingle Bells" by Bing Crosby, one of my favorite classics.

"You make post-Christmas fun," I holler, my face sheepish as I realize the toy is making me speak louder.

LATER...

After surviving an hour of the torments of the toy, I back away from him as he advances towards me. Fully naked, his bare rigid cock swings as he walks.

"You aren't seriously going to also eat my pussy while you do that toy too are you?" Oh, I'm toast now, with butter, jelly, and peanut butter. I'm gone.

"Hell yes, that's what I'm planning." He nods as he backs me up to the backside of the lounge chair.

My jaw drops as he presses a finger to my chest. I fall to the couch saying, "But ..."

"It's just a pussy eating kind of day. What can I say?" He smirks as he kneels before me. "I never said I was only going to use the toy to win."

My jaw falls further as I almost drop the small dough ball still in my hand. I'm about to protest when I realize that would be foolish. "But I have cookie dough. You can't eat me out with cookie dough in my hand."

"I can't? Says who?"

"Mrs. Claus," I shout with desperation, fearing I'm about to lose.

He chuckles as he swirls his thumb in a circle on the phone. My body writhes with each rotation of his thumb towards the top of the screen.

"Uh-huh." He nods with the biggest Cheshire grin ever.

Yep. I'm going to lose. I'm going to lose. I'm going to lose. I am panting.

He is grinning as he nuzzles his nose to part the cleft of my crotch. At first touchdown of his tongue, I cry out. He nudges my thighs apart further with his head.

I twirl the strands of his hair with my free hand, my fingers pressing his scalp when he snakes his tongue under the stem of the toy to lap at my clit. "But," I say with a whimper. "I can't waste this precious dough."

He purses his lips as he stands up. "Okay, babe. I got you." He scoops me up and carries me like a baby back to the kitchen.

"Dump it," he says once we are in the kitchen.

I obey, releasing my tight grip on the dough so it falls to the counter as he sets me down.

I gasp and fall against the cabinet as he sends another series of bursts relentlessly to the toy.

He grips my thighs to steady me. My eyelids roll into a fluttering of my lashes.

I focus on staying standing. It works to stave off my orgasming. My eyes are rolling back and I'm using the counter to keep myself upright.

He kneels down and glances up at me, his eyes full of the priceless passion and lust and love that now delight all my days. He works his fingers over his phone screen rapidly.

My head falls back as a massive moan sprouts out of my lips. My crotch is ready to explode.

He chuckles against my pussy, his mouth full of my lips so the vibration adds to my climbing orgasm. When he pushes his tongue into me alongside the toy I scream out. I've never orgasmed standing up before.

The toy is caressing me on the inside while he is pressing me on the outside. My clit is swollen and sensitive. I'm sure my lips are swollen by now. I cross my fingers as I sink down. Before I even reach the floor, my body is curling, spasming. He lowers me to the floor, cradling me against his head. His phone hits the ground with a clunk before both of his arms shoot up my back. Gently he lays me down as my body twitches over his head, my legs go rigid, my feet curl and stiffen, my soles wrinkle as I scrunch my feet. My arms tighten against his head. With my body fully resting on the hardwood floor, a scream tears out from deep in my lungs. My own sounds shock me as I shake from the convulsions radiating out of my pelvis. I utter strange nonsense words I probably couldn't even spell. My clit is on fire, almost too sensitive to bear against the pressure of his mouth.

I can't even swallow, the scream has hijacked my mouth. I gasp as my body twitches. His arms feel so nice along my butt cheeks as I ride into a second peak of this orgasm. He presses his fingers into my back. His mouth makes slurp sounds to consume my cum as I squirm to get away from him. Locked in place, I writhe as grunts chug out of my mouth.

The spattering of flour to my right catches my eye as I attempt to slow my panting. It looks like the start of snowfall on blacktop, before it is covered in thin sheets of snowflakes making it all white. My elbow falls onto the speckles of flour.

My husband lightly tickles my pussy and thighs with his goatee as I float down from my climax.

"Oh," I sputter, my sighs simmering down to silence. My head lolls to the side on the hardwood floor and I lift it to watch him continue to lap at my groin. I twitch and gasp with each touch of his tongue he presses to my clit. "You are poking the sleeping bear, my love. I've already lost," I whisper.

"No, babe, my beautiful pussy willow, you won."

Well, he's right. But I lost. I resist a shoulder shrug of defeat. I chuckle and shift my hips, but he has me pinned against the cabinets. "You get your wish." Not that I wouldn't have given it to him anyway, but a bet is a bet, and I won't renege. That's a far worse thing than being his plaything.

"I win every day because I have you, babe. You fill my deep emptiness, where I was starving for so long."

The desperation in his voice shouldn't be there, not anymore. Yet it snags at my heart like too many hooks to count, dragging down flesh as it beats.

I raise up on my elbows and look into his watery eyes. "But. You have me and always will." My eyes fill with tears.

His face immediately turns jovial, that twinkle in his eyes that stirs my belly to butterflies, that smile that can turn all my bad days good, his hands that hold me in ways no other man has ... it all hits me like an avalanche. I need him more than he needs me.

"I want you every day. I want to start, middle, and end my day with you and hold you in between." He pulls me onto his lap. "Cradle your heart in my love."

The toy is set on a low hum inside of me, edging me ever so slightly towards the hint of another rise. I lay my head against his cheek as he presses me to his warm chest.

The kitchen is silent, quiet enough to hear us both breathing. The timer goes off.

"I got it," he says as he gently shuffles out from under me.

I settle to the ground and lay flat. My heart still pounding.

The curve of his ass to his thighs looks delicious from below.

"What's so funny?" He glances down at me as he pulls the cookie sheet out of the oven, his smile dancing in his eyes.

"I like this view." I reach for his shins, my grip allowing me to slide myself snug against his lower legs. "I need more of this view." The afterglow of coming so hard has me giddy as I wiggle my head between his legs. "Mmmm, yummy."

His hardon, which seems to be reaching for the counter, sways above me hypnotically as he moves. "These are really beautiful cookies, babe. You did a great job."

"Yeah, especially considering someone kept messing with my pussy," I snicker.

"Where is he? I'll kill him." He jerks his head back and forth feigning looking around for the culprit.

He sets the cookie sheet on the counter and extends his hands down to help me up.

"Oh, I think you'll catch up with him in no time." My arms flop to my sides.

He circles his arms snugly around me and sways us both. The remaining quarter of a dough ball looks rough, all dried out after being open to the air for so long.

"Well, I made a damn good effort. Got through most of that dough before you completely destroyed me." I giggle. "In a good way."

"That you did, babe. That you did."

"You just know how to please me so good that you knew you'd win, didn't you?"

"Oh, I knew you were mine, especially with the toy in you. You were putty in my hands."

"Hell yes. And the only way I ever want it." I tense slightly. "So ... what are you going to choose? Your ultimate unfulfilled fantasy?"

"That, my dear love, is for later today." He holds me tight against his bare skin, the promise of our reaching the point of fucking swollen in every word.

"Oh, the plans you make."

Book 2
The Grocery Store Sex Challenge

"I knew I was going to lose. I had like zero chance with you firing all your artillery, from both the toy and from you. There was a point where I knew my will would definitely collapse." She sighs and blows a breath at the hair on the side of her face. It fluffs out, then settles. "I had no chance at all of not succumbing to all that. It was like an all-out war waged on my pussy!" Her face shows triumph rather than defeat. Anna points to the sex toy on the counter. "But that thing is evil fun."

He waggles his eyebrows as he helps her stand. "It's clean. I did the dishes." Brad picks up the toy and swings it in the air. "Time to reload it, babe."

"Why bother washing it then?" She snickers.

His dumbfounded expression makes her crack up.

"I didn't say I did it with the water from the sink," he says with a big naughty grin, arms outstretched.

"Oh." She smirks and flutters her eyelids.

He leans over her and kisses the top of her head. "Ready? Our day of play continues with our next challenge."

"I can't believe I've agreed to do this in public."

"Spread your legs, babe. Let me in."

Still naked, she raises one leg and holds her thighs open, secured underneath with her hand. The open air hits her moist pussy as a welcome refresh.

"Damn. Are we sure we want to make dinner? I'd rather stay here and play with your pussy." He tickles it with his fingers. "Let's order in instead."

She moans, but then gives him a stern look. "Yes. We need to buy the ingredients. I think it will be fun making dinner from scratch, so let's do it." She sighs as he presses the toy into her still wet womanhood. "Fuck, that feels good. I'm still somewhat aroused." She gives him fuck me eyes.

"Oh, well shit. Now I really want to stay here." He gives her puppy dog eyes.

She lowers her leg. "I need a chance to win with this round, so no canceling."

He sighs. "Okay, let's go." Brad taps his toes while crossing his arms across his broad chest. The whimsical expression on his face is one of many she's come to adore. "I know I'm going to win anyway, so let's do this."

"I hardly see how this is fair at all!" Anna complains as she pulls her pants up. She loses her balance but catches herself by grabbing his arm.

"I think it's perfect." Brad grins and steadies her. "Still a bit wobbly I see. Maybe you should sit down for another minute, babe. Twenty orgasms in a half hour make you a wet noodle."

Anna grins devilishly, then her expression turns goofy as she scoffs. "Perfect for you! You get to play with me with that thing the whole grocery store shopping trip," she says as she points to his phone. She scowls but can't hold her smile as she finishes dressing. "I don't get a remote. We aren't going to be on even playing ground."

He chuckles with a devilish twinkle in his eyes. He points to her crotch. "Nope. I'll be playing with that thing."

Anna rolls her eyes. "Funny thing, this 'thing' is kind of attached to me!" She averts her eyes from making eye contact with him, writes something on her list, crosses it off, then writes something else. "I'm thinking someone needs to invent a male sex toy with a remote to even things out."

Laughing, he peeks at her note. "You think so, huh? Well, we ain't waiting for that to happen. It's game on. Maybe that's your next project."

"Me?" She widens her eyes at him. "Hardly my forte. I'm no engineer." A pulse rages through Anna's pelvis from the toy inside her. She shoots Brad a pained look. "Hey! You said you weren't going to buzz me until we hit the grocery store! You liar!" she accuses, but can't hide her smile from flaring wide and bright.

"Okay, okay. I'll follow the rules." He touches his phone and sends her another pulse. "In a minute," he grumbles.

She smiles as she stands up straight, sticking her breasts out on purpose. With one hand she pulls her shirt over her head, then unclasps her bra with lightning speed. Her breasts swing out. "If we don't follow the rules, it will be total chaos."

"Oh no, now that's not fair at all." He groans as his eyes charge with lust. "You trying to get me to tackle fuck you?" He chortles. "And didn't you just put that shirt and bra on?"

She huffs with a proud expression. "I know how to twist you to your knees."

He chortles. "That you do, babe. That you do." He shakes his head. "Mercilessly."

"I'm just evening the playing field." She shrugs, which makes her breasts jiggle.

He releases a low slow whistle, his right hand migrating up across his forehead and then through his thick hair. "Oh, so you are shopping topless then?" He whoops as he pretends to mess with his phone.

She gives him her best evil eye. "Hardly. But I would If I could. Just to get under your skin." She points at him as she widens her eyes for greater teasing effect. "I'd open the freezer door and just stand there bare-chested, let you watch my nipples gather into their wrinkled peaks."

He clears his throat. "Well, you are getting under my underwear, that's what you are doing." He shakes his hips to show off his erection bulging out the front of his pants. He leans over to peer at her shopping list.

"No peeking!" She flips over the list and gives him an evil eye.

"Exactly why can't I see what we will be buying?" He raises both eyebrows as he tries not to laugh. "I thought we were making this meal together?"

"Cause then you will have a heads up to my scheme. I need some sort of advantage for a plan of attack to get you too, and you not knowing where we are going in the store is all I've got at this point." She huffs as she fumbles with the pen. "This is just not an even fight at all. My disadvantage is maxed out and you've got nothing to push you over the edge." She snatches back up the pen and taps it to her temple as she thinks. Her eyes switch from narrowed to wider as she rotates them from right to left. After a minute, her skeptical look becomes victorious and she says, "Aha! I've got it! I know how I can put you at a disadvantage."

"Shopping topless?" he asks hopefully. "Damn, why isn't that a thing?"

"You are fixating on that. Why don't you invent it?" she asks sarcastically, with significant snark.

"I just might! I'd make a mint. Think how many men would shop there to see bare tits all over the store. That's my heaven, no doubt." He chuckles. "Can you see me at the bank talking to Herman about getting a loan to open a topless grocery store?"

She scowls with an eye flutter. "Well, you'd need to convince the women to shop there." She shoves the pen and shopping list into her open purse, already set right next to her pouch of essential oil roll-ons for on the go. "I'd pay good money to see Herman's expression." She unscrews the cap of the aphrodisiac roll on and coats her neck with it.

Brad taps his lips with his forefinger, which makes Anna want to suck those luscious lips of his into her mouth.

A look of accomplishment spreads across his face. "I've got it! Free stuff!" He rubs his hands together. "Free stuff will be offered to topless women, and only topless women. I'll make so much money on the men that giving away the free stuff will be a wash."

"Hmmmm," Anna says with a raise of an eyebrow. "I can hear the cries of discrimination from the clothed now."

"I'm right, and you know it."

"Maybe," she mutters. "Let's go. I want to shop before I get too hungry for lunch and buy the entire store out."

"Oi, babe, you definitely ain't making it that far," he says as he shakes his phone in her face. "I'm betting we will need to order our meal in."

"Hmpf," she says with a wave of her hand. "I can resist. I'm strong." She heads towards the door out to the garage so she can hide her smile from him. She glances back when he makes an aghast guffaw.

"You riding in the car like that?" he asks with a wanton look.

"Yes," she declares as she returns to the island to grab her shirt and bra in her right hand. "You'd better warm up that car so I don't freeze or I'm blowing you while you drive, and you will lose before we even reach the store."

"Damn! But ...wait ...I want that. Blasted contest!" He throws his arms in the air in defeat.

"Oh. You want to lose, do you?" she asks as she grabs her jacket, then tosses it back down. She points at his face three times to egg him on. She waves her bra and shirt in front of his face. "And this is for the ride home, not the ride there. I'll wait here until you text me." She plops down on the couch.

"I'm on it." He sends her one leering look before he disappears into the garage in a mad scramble.

Anna smacks her lips, sits on the couch, and reads a book on her phone. After ten minutes, she gets the text to come out. As she enters the garage, she shivers. Her nipples go to fully erect mode as she slowly saunters past the front of the vehicle. She shimmies her breasts in the beam of the SUV's headlights.

Her lusty smile taunts him, but her swinging breasts and erect nips are what shove him to the peak of his lust. He had fallen in love instantly with how her breasts firm up when her nipples harden.

Brad shakes his head with a grin. "You are playing hardball," he says as she opens the door.

"Oh, I haven't even started yet, B."

"And you are starting that too. Well, fuck." He releases an exasperated sigh.

She smirks at him and grasps her left nipple and pinches it. She twists it and moans. With a raised eyebrow, she says, "Yes, B."

"Well, fuck," he says. "You are the clever one, aren't you?"

"I know my boob man." She gives him a winner look. "You'd better buck me hard later, B. I'm itching for some pounds after all these pulses."

'B' for Brad, 'B' for boob man, 'B' for buck me. That first night that she had called him 'B', she had been so drunk that she couldn't form words properly. They'd only been dating for three months, but Brad had taught her so much in such a short time. The trust that he had been able to instill in her had blown her mind; she learned quickly and naturally to let him guide her. Being a dominant man with lots of sexual experience, he had led her to such orgasmic heights that she felt swept off her feet just by the sound of his voice, the gentle but firm touch of his hungry hands. The look in his eyes always sealed the deal. She was his. He was hers, but most of all, he held her first in his heart.

That night she had indulged in too much wine and couldn't talk worth anything, so all her words were just the first letter or a drunken garble. She wasn't used to drinking so much and had eaten only a handful of green grapes for lunch, so she got drunk hard and fast. Her horny desires had reached the max point after an hour of foreplay when Brad showed her a new sex toy with a duo attack: a dildo part for inside her pussy and a heavy-duty looking large circular clit sucker. It was shaped like a V and, for some odd reason, she named it Mary upon sight. Brad had practically rolled off the couch when she named it, then roared even harder when she begged to be 'bucked' by Mary.

She shakes the lovely memory off with a head jerk and grasps her right nipple with her free hand. Time to focus on now. She plays with both nipples at the same time and leans her head against the seat as her eyes roll back in her head. "Mmmm. Damn. This feels amazing."

He grumbles something she can't make out, then sighs as he starts to back up the vehicle. He chortles as his cock fills his pants further, stretching the log of his erection against the ungiving fabric. "Umpf," he mutters. Shifting in his seat does not relieve the discomfort one bit. "Well, you aren't that smart because I know how much that arouses you too, so your moves are serving to edge us both."

She frowns and presses her lips together in a firm line. "Quit pooh-poohing my tactics. I know what I'm doing."

He pauses at the end of the driveway, glancing around to see if any pedestrians could see Anna topless – not that he cares. Actually, he finds it rather hot to contemplate. He loves showing off his beautiful, sexy wife. "Okay. Ground rules. We make the rules now and can't change them once we both agree on them." He sneaks a peek at her again and groans.

"Okay. Agreed." Anna plays with her nipples more and gives them both a tug. She bemoans exaggeratedly.

"Dammit," he mutters as his desire for her rages more. He clears his throat, his hands gripping the wheel to the point of white knuckles. He clears his throat again. It's not working to reduce the pressure in his cock, nor to lessen his lust. He backs into the street and proceeds through their neighborhood. "No touching each other in the store." He can't keep himself from glancing over at her again as she's molesting her tits; he wants his fingers where her fingers are playing.

"Eyes on the road, Romeo. You are supposed to be driving, B," she scolds happily.

"You aren't playing fair this time." His lower lip slips out in a pout.

"Keep spewing rules, B. I'm busy with my nipples," she says in a hushed yet commanding tone, accentuating the end of the sentence seductively.

He puffs out a scoff. "You know how bad I want to do that."

"You bet your ass I do, lover boy. Next rule." She chuckles before releasing a series of exaggerated moans.

"Wow," he says with desperation. "That's fucking driving me crazy."

"I know," she whispers while giving him fuck me eyes.

"Oh, not the look too!" He releases a pained sigh. "Fuck. Fuck. Fuck. If we weren't in the middle of this challenge, I'd pull over and fuck you on a side road. You know that, right?"

"Uh-huh," she says in a low, singsong voice. "Next rule," she demands in a soft tone, her words coming out like a pleasant hum.

"Whoever either orgasms first or begs for more in the store loses. And losing means another fantasy gets fulfilled." He pauses as he contemplates. "Or sexual favor granted on demand."

"Oh, a new addition." She nods as she continues to play hard with her nipples, despite turning herself on almost to the edge of orgasm. "Okay, I'm in," she says breathlessly. She acknowledges that she's still at a serious disadvantage in this challenge. If she could just touch his cock, she knows he'd come in the store, and she'd win. Instead, she will have a toy nudging and vibrating her clit and G-spot. She sighs. She will likely lose. Again. She catches the eyes of a truck driver passing by. He sits just slightly above the SUV so he can see exactly what she is doing. His eyes widen, so she smiles at him. He smiles back.

She shifts her gaze to Brad. He grits his teeth as she tugs at her hard, thick nips, pulling them as far from her body as she can, even to slight pain.

"Fuckkkkk me," he slurs with want. He knits his brow into a deep furrow and his lower lip protrudes once more as he firms his top lip.

Anna suppresses a chuckle beneath her greedy grin. "I'm good with all of that. And no protesting from either of us. Whatever happens, we can't complain." She's never seen him pout like this before and she's loving it.

"Oh, that will be tough for you."

"You just wait," she mutters. "Do we have any more rules?" She grins wickedly.

"I think that's it. Unless you have something to add."

"Nope. I'm good if you are." She pushes her hand into her pants and plays with her pussy lips.

He glances at her and gasps deeply. "Hey! Not playing fair!" he exclaims.

"Oh, wait. I do have another stipulation. You can't touch my nipples until we are back home."

He cringes. "Not even on the way home?" he asks with frustration, like she just took his last bite of the best steak of his life.

"Nope." She sniggers with glee as his pouting expression intensifies. "It's only fair. I will be touched by the toy the whole time in the store and nothing but your pants are touching your cock. This evens things out some."

"But ..." He gives her serious, weepy, poor me eyes.

"It's non-negotiable."

He grunts like a kid denied a donut.

"Pout all you want. That's my contribution to this challenge." She rubs her clitoris and releases sounds of pleasure.

"Fuck. This really sucks. Fuck! I've literally signed up for torment and blue balls!"

"Deal?" she demands with pursed lips and narrowed eyes.

"Fine. Deal. I can't resist you. But I'm totally roasting that pussy. No holding back," he declares with passion, mirroring his eyes to hers in slits as he peers intently at her.

"Okay. I agree." She sighs softly and whimpers as she continues to play with her right nipple and her wet folds.

He stops the car at a stoplight. "Why do I feel like I just signed a deal with the devil?" He glances at her nervously. "And I thought I was golden to win this round."

She unclicks her seatbelt. "Not even close." She rises up on her knees and leans down towards his lap.

"Wait ... wait ... wait ... what are you doing? You can't do this. I win by default. You can't touch."

She snickers. "We said no touching in the store." A wide triumphant smile spreads across her face. "Not the car. And it's only you can't touch my nipples. Pay attention, B."

"Oh shit. This is cheating! You trapped me."

"No, it's not. It fits our agreed-upon rules."

"I'm in deep shit now, aren't I?" His grin that reaches his eyes tells her he wants this, despite the outcome.

She unzips his pants while keeping eye contact with him. His eyes shift between her and the road on repeat.

"You are in deep something. I know how fast you came last time I gave you road head topless." She smacks her mouth by opening and closing it quickly, and then makes kissing sounds. "Remember?"

He releases a slow sigh. He's fucked. "Well played," he whispers as she takes his cock in her hand and strokes it.

She seals her mouth around his cockhead and begins to suck while stroking his shaft.

He groans deeply as she runs her tongue under his cockhead ridge and caresses his frenulum with the tip of her tongue.

"Oh, fuck me," he groans out. "My fingers are on fire to fondle you. It's literally killing me to not touch you." He rolls out a long, low, impatient groan. "Remind me to never underestimate you again," he manages to say with great effort.

She hums with his cockhead in her mouth.

He slams on the car brakes and her head hits the steering wheel.

"Ow!" she exclaims as she scrambles to steady her body. She rubs her head where she smacked into the steering wheel.

"Fuck the giblets! Shit!" he screams. "I almost hit that car. This is a really bad idea."

"Is it?" she teases before taking him back into her mouth. She giggles as she rubs her pinkie and thumb slowly along his shaft so her other fingers can glide along as she strokes him. She slides her mouth off his swollen cock head. "You sure are packed tight right now, B. You must be ready to blow." She hovers over his erection, ensuring her hot breath bathes his taut skin before she devours his cock.

Her calling him 'B' brings up such hot memories of the night of him rage fucking her to her cries for more, plus, her orgasming at a rate of almost an orgasm a minute. Then, add in his reduced faculties as he tries to drive safely and, with all that, he fears he's surely a goner. About to lose before they even reach the store, he pounds the wheel with both palms as she sighs deeply. She comes off his cock for a few seconds, her parted lips just bobbing above his erection. The tease is agonizing. He tries to squirm her off his lap as his grimace deepens. He struggles to control his urge to ejaculate.

He gasps as his arousal stabilizes. "Whew, I almost lost it, almost spewed my whole load there. Way too hard to not come and not hit a car at the same damn time."

His heavy panting is turning her on more.

She was unlike any other woman he'd ever been with, being that she was so free sexually, he learned early on in their relationship that he could guide her to places of extreme pleasure neither of them dreamt possible. All of it, all of her, is his dream come true.

She clears her throat before blowing a hot breath on the stretched skin of his erection. "Fuck the giblets? Hmm. One more dash of salt." She takes his cockhead back in her mouth and sucks hard.

He grunts heartily and fidgets in the seat, trying to shake her off. "This is just brutal." He gasps and his whole body tenses. "Wet dog shit filled yard after winter. Maggots on stinky steak. Day-old fish heads and guts in a bucket, topped with expired tartar sauce and a side of moldy ... oh, I don't know what." He groans again as he presses his hips back into the seat. "Ack! Help!"

She laughs with his full penis head in her mouth. She pops off of him and cracks up.

He doesn't slow as he speeds into the parking lot. The SUV hits a speed bump and flies up.

"Oh," Anna exclaims as the jolt of the vehicle sends her body into the air. She plops back on his lap as the car levels off. "Whoa!"

Brad gasps before he says, "Thank Gawd we're here. I couldn't resist that for much longer."

"Driving like a maniac, B. You should be more careful." She winks at him as he presses his foot slowly on the brake. "I almost had you."

"No shit you did. That was the toughest resist ever in my whole life." He shakes his head with a grimace. "Just you topless gets me almost all the way there all by itself, babe."

"I know my sexual charms," she says in a huff as she caresses her breasts with both hands.

"Ya, you do," he mutters.

Once they pull into a parking spot, Anna puts on her shirt, but places her bra on the dash. The large pale pink domes of its cups almost glow against the dark of the car's interior.

He flares his eyes wide at her as he shifts his gaze back and forth between the bra and her. "Oh, fuck me. You are going to shop braless?" His words come out incredulous, as if he's just been given a car for free only to have it taken back.

She smiles smugly. "Yup. Part of my weaponry is you will have to watch my girls bounce as I shop."

"Oh shit. I'm in big trouble," he says with emphasis on 'big.'

"You just wait." She hops out of the car.

"And you know how I love to show you off, you sexy minx." He exits the vehicle and quickly struts to the back of the car, wiggling his hips, trying to relieve some of the pressure his pants are forcing on his erection. Why didn't he wear the loose-fit jeans today? "Aren't you the smart one?"

She winks. "Just the first of my many tricks." She scuttles in front of him and pulls her leggings tight up her ass crack.

He groans. "Oh, come on. Not the ass and camel toe too," he mutters as he sets the lock on the vehicle with a press of the button on the key fob.

Anna shivers against the brutal wind but flips around and walks backward so he can get a full visual of her hardened nipples beneath her shirt.

"Oh, my Gawd," he whispers in a strained voice, like she's got her hands on his balls. Which, basically, she does. "I want to devour you."

"Come get me," she says with a shudder and a naughty grin. "Yours for the taking." She grabs her breasts and squeezes them. She glances around in hopes that someone is watching.

"You're gonna trip walking backward like that," he chides.

"I'm being careful," she says in an uppity tone, just as she hits an icy spot that throws her off balance. "Oh!" she exclaims as she raises her arms in the air.

Brad rushes a step forward and grabs her by the arm. "I've got you." He pulls her close in a hug, crushing her breasts to his chest.

"Whoa! Shit! You saved me." Her face goes from terror to love as her expression softens. "Thank you, lover."

"My pleasure. I've always got you."

"I know," she whispers with warmth in her eyes. Her eyes turn to flirt mode. "And you just touched my breasts, but I'll let that go since you saved me from an ass bruise."

He kisses the top of her head, then whispers, "Let's go shop."

Her eyes mirror his love.

He wraps an arm around her shoulders and pulls her close.

She sighs as she leans on his shoulder with another shiver. "Brrrr." She tries to calm her shaking body but fails. "And the not touching begins once we are in the store."

"You've got to be freezing. I'll try to keep you warm." He snuggles her closer as they make their way towards the door. They can't shuffle fast enough, and her body convulses violently.

Once inside the door, Anna rushes to the warmth with an appreciative sigh while Brad grabs a shopping basket. He approaches Anna, who is inspecting the grapes.

"We don't need a cart, right? We aren't getting much, are we?"

"Nope, a basket is perfect." Yep. Perfect. Her plan is in motion already.

"Want some grapes?" he asks eyeing them up.

"Nah, I was just looking. I think we still have some at home." She wanders over towards the asparagus. Grapes aren't on the list.

Brad wastes no time and pulls out his phone. He drags his fingers across it to set it vibrating inside her. He smiles, deeply enjoying watching as she jerks, then gasps. Her pretty mouth parts into an oval as a sweet sigh escapes her lips. He loves those little mewls she makes.

"Oh, already?" she mutters as she recovers from the blast to her groin. She smiles as she grabs a bunch of asparagus. She turns and he zaps her again. "Oh, fuck," she whispers as she tries to hide the shock on her face, glancing around to see if anyone is in earshot. "That was a strong one."

"Oh, I intend to win, babe. I owe you from the car ride." He takes the vegetables from her hands and plops them in the basket. "You shop, I'll buzz you."

She can't help but love the joy on his face, even if it's to her sexual torment. He sends two bursts her way as more happiness erupts from his eyes.

Her body convulses and she looks around again to see who is watching her. "Humpf. Hardly seems fair at all," she complains then presses her lips together. She realizes she's complaining and holds her breath to see if it registers with him. She may have to rearrange her game plan. Brad needs a handicap, some sort of hindrance or she's going to lose this round fast. "Mushrooms," she mutters under her breath. "Quick quick quick," she chants as she almost runs to the mushrooms. "Hurry," she mutters to herself.

He sends a series of pulses to the toy. She comes to a complete stop in her tracks. Her torso curls forward in response to the heavy barrage of jolts zinging through the toy inside her pussy. "Omigod," she says with several gasps and heaves of her chest as she tries to not yell out.

She turns to the cucumbers and grabs one as her body is still twitching from the all-out war he's set upon her pussy. She confirms Brad is in full sight of her because she needs him looking for this move. She shoves the cucumber between her breasts and presses her biceps together like she's going to titty fuck the phallic vegetable. She rubs it up in her cleavage, not caring a lick who the fuck is watching.

His jaw drops. "Oh, well fuck," he whispers. "You are playing super hardball."

Her smile turns impish. "Calls the devil with the devil on his shoulder and a pussy tickler on his phone!" She glances down and her nipples are still poking out of her shirt. Perfect. That'll get him going hot and heavy.

An older gentleman in a thick ski jacket and maroon and gold stocking cap grins at them. "Howdy, Brad. Anna."

Anna's face immediately flushes as she realizes it's George from their gym.

"Hey, George," Brad says with a sheepish grin.

Anna yanks the cucumber from her cleavage, her cheeks deepening her blush.

"Going to buy that one, eh?" George chuckles heartily. "Having some fun at the grocery store, huh? Makes my heart smile to see you two. Always playful. Kind of like Marnie and me, only way bolder." He hefts a hearty laugh. "Though I'd pay good money to watch her do what you just did, sweetheart."

Anna drops the unneeded cucumber into Brad's basket and then grabs another to add to it, even though cucumbers are not on the list. "One for later too," Anna jokes as she suppresses the urge to literally run away.

"That's a girl," George says with the biggest grin.

Anna surmises he's a good sport. Vegetable to tits isn't an everyday grocery store sight. She leaves the men to their small talk and makes her way as calmly as possible to the salad section. She snatches up a bag of butter lettuce and a bag of croutons on display to her left, without even looking at the flavor. Then, without waiting for Brad, who is still incessantly chatting with George about the weather, she hustles along to the pasta aisle. She's pleased her plan is working so far. Let him scramble to catch up. Her breasts swing loose and free as she rushes. She loves the feeling of the shirt against her bare skin. She's enjoying this even more as she passes a young man who gives her a big smile.

"Morning," he says with a glance at her chest.

She smiles back. "Good morning." As she hurries past a few other men, who all smile at her, she silently giggles. Boob men are slaves to the almighty erect nipple.

A woman passes by her with a smirk. "Nice shirt," she says with a raise of her eyebrow.

This time Anna doesn't blush but smirks back. "Why, thank you." She is grateful she doesn't recognize the woman, and that she has a pleasant expression. Not that she really cares though.

In the pasta aisle, she picks up a jar of alfredo sauce, contemplating buying it as a backup in case their homemade sauce turns out inedible. A very real possibility with all this sexual play distracting her. Who can cook properly with pussy tickles? She turns the jar around to read the back label just as Brad sends the strongest pulses possible in a barrage. She gasps and arches her back as the jar slips out of her hand. It smashes on the floor with a loud crack, sending shoots of white sauce everywhere. Unfortunately, he leaves the toy on high mode. She drops the bag of croutons and the mushrooms as she focuses on not crushing the bag of lettuce to her chest.

"Oh shit!" she exclaims under her breath as she fights against showing the people nearby what the toy is doing to her pussy. "Dammit, Brad! Bad timing." Her face flushes as she fights her body twitches.

An older woman nearby says, "Honey, are you okay? Don't worry. I'll get a worker for you, love. Don't worry, please, hon." Her face softens sweetly. "It happens to us all."

Anna sighs. The woman probably thinks she's having a seizure. Or is just a mega klutz. Well, not really, nice old lady. Most people don't shop with a toy in their pussy. Brad, please stop, she silently begs. She takes a step forward to try and disguise the forces her clit is sending through her body.

With already pleading eyes, she sees Brad appear at the end of the aisle. His face falls as he rushes to Anna. He stops dead in his tracks and taps his phone screen.

The vibrations stop and Anna's body relaxes.

Oops, he went too far.

Overcome with emotion, his face shows chagrin. "Oh, babe. I'm sorry. And with a glass jar too." He shakes his head as he glances at his phone to ensure it's off. "Shit. My bad, babe. Sorry." He chastises himself for teasing her hard when she wasn't under his watchful eyes. He rubs her arm and cradles her to him in a side hug, carefully avoiding her delectable breasts. "We're in this together," he says softly.

"Your timing sucks. And you are touching me," she mutters as she bites her lip. A laugh threatens to bubble out of her mouth. "Was going to buy that for a backup in case our sauce tanks, but you've changed my mind." The laugh finally slips out.

"I see that. I'll go get someone to clean this up."

Anna raises her hand to stop him.

A worker in a black apron scampers to them with a mop and bucket in his hands. "Hey. I've got this. No worries." He is the perfect customer service dude without an inkling of anger. "Happens at least once every other day."

"I'm sorry," Anna says sincerely. She smacks Brad on the chest. Her face transforms quickly into mock anger. "He made me do it."

Brad lets out a belly laugh before saying, "She's not wrong. We'll pay for it."

The worker waves his hand in the air. "Nah, don't worry about it."

"Well, I want to, it is my fault." Brad looks Anna in the eyes, their mischievous intent very evident if the man were to look. "I was messing with her, so I made it happen."

Anna widens her eyes. "Oh, it's called messing now, is it?"

Brad's eyes flicker with joy. "Yep. That's one word for it." He leans over and picks up the croutons and mushrooms. "But I have much better words for it."

"You beast," she whispers as she creeps past Brad, realizing the worker likely heard her when a little smile grows across his face. "Thank you. Again, I'm sorry for the mess," she says to him, trying to cover up her saucy attitude.

"No sauce, then?" Brad asks in a teasing voice.

"Shut it, chef," she mocks back. "This way, B." She points towards the back of the store.

"You won't stop with that, will you?"

She shakes her head and glances back at him. "Nope." She releases an exasperated guffaw. "B." She sighs deeply. "I've never dropped a jar in the store in my life. Now I'm one of those people!" She shoots him a nasty look, but then smiles. "You are in for it, mister." She shakes her finger at him. "No holds barred."

The delight on his face spreads to his twinkling eyes. "I wouldn't want it any other way, babe. Lay it on me thick as you want." This game with her puts him in heaven.

She purses her lips and heads straight for the freezer section, without hesitation.

He chuckles as he follows behind her, phone raised, finger poised at the ready for relentless pussy tickling action. He's definitely winning this round. There is no doubt in his mind. He sends her a series of strong pulses, the kind he knows drives her crazy wild.

She walks like she's dancing, but she fears she looks more like she's jerking from ants biting her skin. He ramps up the power of the little toy and she twitches like she's walking on hot fire, with muffled cries escaping her lips. She glares at him. "I must look like I'm getting shock therapy."

"Well, you are!" He can't keep the grin off his face.

Her facial expression flickers between annoyance and scheming. "You are enjoying this way too much!" She flings open the freezer door and leans in. Her nipples harden further.

"Mmmm. Whoa." He moans. "Oh, well I'm enjoying that even more."

She shimmies her shoulders so her breasts swing in the cool air spilling out of the upright freezer, her erect nipples riding arousingly back and forth against her shirt.

He lets out a slow low groan. "Damn. Fuck me, it's like a wet t-shirt contest in that shirt."

"I know, why do you think I picked it?" She refuses to admit she didn't think of that before but is super glad now. She shakes her breasts in the freezer, occasionally glancing around to see if anyone is watching her shake her tits in the cold mist. She'd have serious explaining to do if she saw a friend or someone from work. But that is part of the naughty fun too. "I want you to suck my nipples, B. Please. I want you to run your tongue all over my areola creases, dips, and bumps. Feel me up with your mouth and tongue. Make my nipples ready to cut glass." She moans seductively. "I need a titty fuck right now."

He releases a slow whistle. "Well, shit. I'm hard as a rock, babe. With that, I'm definitely your love slave."

He reaches for his phone as she watches, holding her breath. She presses her lips together bracing for the onslaught of pulses she knows he will send. To her surprise, he gives it to her real slow, in light pulses. She blows out the breath she's been hoarding.

"Mmm, that feels so nice, B," she murmurs. "Want you to fuck me right here, right now."

"I want to touch you so bad right now, Anna." His voice comes out almost as a whine. He coughs as he glances at his cock pressing out his jeans. "You have no idea." He's super grateful he has his long coat on to sort of hide his arousal.

He increases the strength of the toy's pulsing.

Anna's eye pop open wide. She hums and wiggles her body, savoring the feeling of the vibrations traveling her female parts. "Being here reminds me of when we had sex on the beach and people were walking along the shore nearby. Remember the cool breeze off the ocean as we made each other come on the sand?"

"Yes, babe. And how I ate you out to the sound of the waves? The moonlight glistening off your sexy fine breasts, your skin just glowed in that light." Dammit if he might just come in his pants.

"Mmmm, all those stars overhead. I can see it now," she says dreamily as she sways with her hands still gripping the freezer door frame stabilizing her. "Was a magical night, B."

"Yeah, that's right. It was epic." He clears his throat to try and shake off his desire for her.

Her giggle ends in a scoff. "Yeah, because it was unforgettable."

"Yes. That's the first time I made you have a multiple peaked orgasm." At the time, neither of them had thought her body would gift her six peaks. His face shifts to an evil grin as he blasts the toy on high. "It's okay babe, I wanna make you come right now. It will be so hot. Come for me, babe. Right here. Right now, come for me," he whispers into her hair covered ear from above.

Memories of their first getaway flood her brain as her body slips helplessly into orgasm mode. It had been way too soon to go out of town with him, he had been practically a stranger. But after only three dates, he had invited her to Key West, Florida, to stay at a resort. Her daughter had panicked when she said she was going away with her new boyfriend, but Anna had known from the beginning that Brad was her perfect life partner. His immediate concern for her well-being, her pleasure, her happiness hinted at love before the word even dared to dance into her mind. Then, when he had first said the magic three words it had shocked her, but it was as if she'd almost known it already. Plus, he had made her pancakes while she slept that first morning of their getaway. No man had ever made her breakfast while she still slept. What they had was special and she knew it from the very start.

Her body begins the usual orgasm curl as she widens her eyes, closes them, then her torso suddenly goes rigid. "Oh, shit, I know what you are doing you sneaky devil you. You are seducing me with orgasm memories," she struggles to say. She takes several slow breaths in to calm herself. "Not going to be that easy, B." She shakes her head and then straightens up, regaining composure.

"Dang it!" he says way too loud. "I almost had you."

She snickers. "Nope. Not gonna happen, fucker." Though she's not admitting he's right.

His face contorts aghast. "Fucker? Hey, I was pleasuring you."

"No, you were winning!" She turns hard and fast which makes her pendulous braless orbs swing and shake before they settle as she freezes in place.

"Whew, I seriously cannot think while looking at you without a bra on, even when your luscious breasts are under a shirt." He fans himself.

She shuts the freezer door. "Now that was a close one." She nods, now reserved and stoic. "On with the business at hand. We need milk." She nods at a man who apparently had watched them the whole time, the evidence is all over his grin and horny eyes.

"Afternoon," he says with a nod, his lips set in an excited grin.

"Afternoon," Brad says with a tone of knowing what's going through his mind.

"Great day for fun games," he says with a hint of praise. "Might have to copy that game myself." He does the cliché rapid eyebrow raise.

Anna averts her eyes, so he doesn't see her eye roll.

"Oh, you should. Totally. It's the best one out there." Brad's voice cracks as he coughs. "This app makes it all fun."

The man chuckles. "Oh, one of those new thingamajigs. Just need to convince the wifey." He tilts his head upward and points to a heavy-set woman way at the other end of the aisle who is peering into the freezer intently.

"I have faith in you." Brad pats his bicep. "The more pleasure the better, my man."

"Oh, and don't I know it." He drops a bag of frozen fries in his cart. "Have a good day you two."

"You as well," Brad says with a nod. Brad almost places his hand on her back out of sheer habit. "Live life to the fullest, my man."

Anna sniffs. She has no words. "Milk, Brad. Let's get milk." She'll show him who's going to win.

"What?" he asks exasperated, pulled from the guy talk too early.

"Male bonding over sex toys, now I've seen it all." Her voice is laced with fake disgust as she tries not to laugh.

He mirrors her with a belly laugh. "What? If I can help a man out, I'm going to."

"You mean a woman?"

"Well, both, my love. Both get pleasure out of such inventions." He beams at her with a bright smile. "I could be their poster boy and get lots of sales." He points to his giant grin.

"Milk," she commands beguilingly as she points towards the back of the store and leads him that way, head down as if going into a hard rain.

"We are skipping around the store in an ineffective manner."

"Quit being a damn engineer," she spits. "I'm following my artist bone. And is that a complaint?"

"Oh, you said bone," he says suggestively with a juvenile heckle. "I have that." He sends Anna a low buzz to edge her.

The dairy area is highly congested with shoppers.

"Yeah, I want your bone. Should we just do it on the floor right here?" She dances about as she suggestively bites her lip.

"If we want to go to jail tonight!" He cocks his head. "But I'd say no, because they won't put us in the same cell and that means no fucking." His expression goes haughty as he shakes his head. "Sex in a jail cell, that would be new."

"Guess that wouldn't bode well for our game, now would it?" She glances around, realizing other shoppers are close enough to hear their conversation.

"Nope," he says. "Afraid not."

The woman nearby grabbing coffee creamer makes eye contact as she laughs.

"Sorry," Anna says quickly.

"Oh, don't be," she says with a knowing smile, her eyes a brilliant blue. "Though I wouldn't recommend jail sex," she jokes.

Anna and Brad both guffaw.

A couple next to them frowns, but it only serves to make Anna laugh harder. All the sensations flooding her sensitive womanhood has her feeling a bit drunk and careless.

She opens the door to the dairy case and selects a gallon of milk after too much contemplation. She spins and plops it hard in Brad's basket, disrupting his ability to finish what he had been about to do on his phone.

"Oof," he says as his body is pulled forward by the unexpected weight of the milk in his basket. He grunts. "What? A full gallon? Since when do we need a full gallon? Unless the kids are coming over."

She purses her lips before she says, "Well, they might." She smiles smugly. "We need a gallon. Or two." She reaches in the fridge and snatches another one. She plops it in his basket and it almost falls right back out, so he has to cradle the big load to his body.

"Ugh. Well, this will make things interesting." He clears his throat as he attempts to find an easy way to hold the heavy basket and his phone up at once. "These cold areas of the store are sure wreaking havoc on me."

She smiles knowingly. "Well, the sauce aisle didn't work out so great for me." She spins away from him.

He had known early on in their relationship they'd end up like this, sexually playful. He had felt their spark the second they had met, not that he had known fully, but there was just something about the way she looked at him, even right from the start. There was something magical in her eyes. She had the kind of eyes that were both filled with naughty fun and sweetness at once. She was a beautiful woman, but that held nothing to the beauty and love in her heart. And with her smart brain to boot, he had been rightly smitten. Not that he believed in love at first sight, but it had been something at first sight.

Within minutes of first being around her, he knew it, even if he couldn't have explained it at the time. Something he couldn't even fathom but held on to fiercely because such jewels rarely surfaced twice in life. He wasn't letting her go for anything.

He needs to step up his game if he's going to win this round though. With the milk jugs in his basket weighing his other hand down, he will have to use his thumb to control the toy with the same hand he's holding his phone with, which is going to be extremely difficult, if not impossible.

"Okay, let's get the cheeses." She scampers ahead with youthful jubilance, almost skipping. She hums like she's galloping through a field of daisies.

Brad laughs as he struggles both to hold the full basket and press his phone to taunt her with the toy. It's not possible. He threads his arm deeper through the basket's handles. The whole thing presses heavily on the crook of his arm. He tries to hold the phone with his hand on the arm holding the basket and uses his free hand to try to manipulate the toy on the screen. With great effort, he manages to tap the right spot.

Anna halts her movement and lets out a little screech. "Fuck," she mutters under her breath.

Brad grins hugely as he moves his fingers around the phone screen, maneuvering a fingertip deftly to bring her to the levels of arousal he wants her at.

She fights through her lust and grabs two packets of cheese, which she promptly plops in his basket. She grins big as she snatches the large cottage cheese container from the shelf. Then she grabs another, and a two-pound pack of butter. She hefts them all into Brad's basket, but they don't fit so he's forced to use his other hand to secure them.

"Balls," he says with a puffy breath. "We need two of each?" he asks incredulously. One cottage cheese container almost falls out, but he rights it just in time. "I need more hands."

She tilts her head with an eyebrow raise. "I'm feeling like I need lots for breakfasts. Craving it." She eyes up the largest block of cheddar in the case and wraps her fingers around it with a triumphant grin, knowing it won't fit and Brad will completely lose the use of his free hand for pressing his phone screen. He will be rendered useless to tease her any longer. She will win! Or at least it will be a draw, but that's not losing. She snickers. This is the first time she's ever considered an orgasm to be losing.

She plops the big cheese on top and he grunts. "Who is going to eat all this cheese?" He attempts to shift his phone and drops it when a screaming running toddler plows into him. The little blond boy zooms away, giggling as his mom scolds him.

"Oh, shitake!" He watches as his phone smacks face down on the hard ground. "Mushroom," he manages to blurt out in a depressed tone.

"Oh no!" she exclaims as she stoops to pick it up. The bending down action presses the toy's vibrating parts harder against her sensitive areas, making the sensation more intense. She gasps as she struggles to stand up. She turns the phone over to examine the screen. "Oh, it's okay. Thank goodness." She's begun to pant. She waves her hand at the basket dismissing his protest. "No harm done. And, oh, cheese lasts. For months. Don't worry. We'll eat it," her words come out between breathy panting. She almost rubs her hands together. Her plan is working though. "You have so much to carry, maybe I should carry your phone for you."

"Now I know why you wanted a basket instead of a cart." He screws his face into a painful look, which transforms quickly into an 'aha' look. "Be right back. I'll find you. I'll just listen for the screams," he taunts. He bearhugs the basket to his chest and barrels off down the aisle, dodging people like he's a video game character.

"Ha ha," she calls after him. "Very funny." He'd better not try ticking her pussy from afar again.

He dashes off to his left at the end of the aisle for the front of the store. Two can play at on-the-fly scheming. He makes his way past the candy but stops to snag a bag of dark chocolates. He struggles to shove the corner of the bag between his teeth and bites down hard. To gain a further notch towards winning, he'd dangle Anna's favorite kind of chocolate in front of her, entice her into more moans. It is worth a try.

With the basket handles pressing deeply into the skin of his arm, he practically jogs to the entrance of the store despite the heavy load. He's desperately hoping he doesn't set off any alarms as he crosses the threshold of the entrance. Alarms blare immediately as he lumbers along struggling to not drop anything.

"Dammit," he mutters. The bag of chocolates falls to the floor, landing with a clunk. An old lady covers her mouth as her eyes widen, a little boy next to her holding her hand giggles.

"Sorry," he offers as he finally sets the heavy basket down. He cringes as he rushes to grab the cart. He needs to work as fast as he can so he can get back into the store, and hopefully lift the trigger of the alarm. He picks up the basket and several items fall out and smack on the ground. The cottage cheese container cracks and white liquid oozes out.

"Fuck, I mean fudge," he mutters under his breath, glancing several times at his audience. But to no avail, the little boy and the old lady heard, their respective expressions deepening. He grabs the sanitizing wipes and quickly swipes up the mess. He loads it all into the cart at hyper speed. Damn! He's sweating.

He nods to his shocked onlookers and hustles away, feeling guilty that he jarred a grandma immobile and swore in front of a child.

While pushing the cart into the store, he spots the store manager, whom he knows, coming his way. It's his friend, Mustafa. He waves. "My bad, just needed a cart." He glances around apologetically at the other shoppers. "I'm the store freak today, sorry folks."

"Hey, Brad." He and Mustafa had been on a church rec baseball team several decades ago. Mustafa taps something on his phone and blissfully the alarm stops, allowing Brad to sigh in relief. "No worries on that. I get it. That lovely new wife of yours loading you down too much?" His look is knowing yet approving.

He gives his friend an expression of pleasant relief. "Yep. She's on a shopping spree when we had only planned to buy one meal." He balances the basket in the child seat and unloads the remainder of the groceries into the cart.

"Always happens, doesn't it?" He chuckles. "We grocery store managers bank on that." He pats Brad on the shoulder. "How's married life treating you?"

"Fabulous." He grins so big he feels his cheeks might break. "We are wreaking havoc in your store today though."

"Ah, bah. This stuff happens daily. It's the norm," he says with a dismissive wave of his hand, the smile never leaving his face.

"Oh, I bet. Never a dull moment, huh?"

"Nope. People shop all times of the day, even at night." He glances at his phone. "Well, congratulations. I'll let you get back to her. I've got another issue to handle."

"Nice to see you." Brad releases a big sigh.

"Likewise." Mustafa waves as he rushes off.

Once Brad has the load nicely settled into the cart, he turns his attention to Anna's pussy, via his phone. He manipulates the little controls to high and then grimaces. The jar of sauce incident stops him. He shouldn't play aggressively when he can't see her. He drops the level of the toy down to low and makes his way to where he last saw her.

After passing three quarters of the aisles, he spots Anna. As he approaches, her face contorts with humor. "That alarm was you, wasn't it?" She cracks up. "Serves you right!"

He grins sheepishly. "Afraid so."

"They are going to chase us out of the store at this rate." She shakes her head in bemusement.

"No doubt. Saw Mustafa."

"Nice. How is he?"

"Good. He's the one who stopped the store alarm when he saw it was me." He taps the phone to bring the toy's pulsing to near maximum power. "Oh, there goes that devil on my shoulder again. He's naughty."

She ignores him. "We need to go back for the meat."

He pulses the toy even higher, just under max power. "Meat, you say?" he asks suggestively.

Her body undulates, she can't even chuckle at his joke. She falls silent.

"Yeah. We kind of skipped the meat when you ran for the freezer section." His eyes drift down to her erect nipples, which literally haven't stopped poking out her shirt the entire shopping trip. "I've got the ideal meat for you." He leans down to her ear and whispers, "Going to bend you over that stack of pop cans and fuck you from behind. Ram my hard cock into you so hard you scream."

She glances at his erection at full mast again and pretends to melt to the floor.

He's not wasting that, real or fake. He ramps up the power of the sex toy to the maximum level.

Her sinking body twitches, then writhes in the air as her eyelids flutter involuntarily, then roll back in her head. She recovers for a second to give him a look of utter surprise, a look he finds delicious. Next, it's an expression of extreme vulnerability he cherishes every time he sees it.

She shakes as the rise to her climax rages closer to culmination. Having been edged for the last twenty-five minutes, she's a goner. Surprised at her own loss of inhibitions, she loses all control as her clit takes it and pushes her ever nearer to the edge of the apex. Pleasure mixes with fear as her panic rises. Who will see her like this? Hopefully not anyone she knows. The power of her body takes her to that place she's powerless to resist. It's not about claiming the orgasm when it claims first. This is something she had learned with Brad. The art of orgasming is about letting go. Now it just happens naturally for her, so much so that stopping it isn't even an option anymore. The pulsations radiating out from her crotch act like strings of a puppet as her body begins to scrunch up, curling in on itself. Her fingers curl into claws, her knees begin to buckle, and she fears she might literally fall. But that doesn't stop the blossoming of her orgasm. She never thought it'd happen, but here she is succumbing to having an orgasm in public.

Brad drops his phone into the cart, overcome with emotion he cannot resist, he cradles her against his body. He catches her as she fully collapses into him while twitching. A soft moan escapes her mouth, and he recognizes she's using extreme restraint in order to not scream out. He envelopes his wife fully, so their fronts smash together as she submits, allowing her orgasm to play out.

His heart swells as she lays her head against his chest, eyes closed but eyelids still fluttering as she finishes the climb to the high.

"Babe. You look beautiful," he whispers as he enjoys the intimate show. He can't ever get enough of watching her come.

She falls silent. This is the part he really loves when she loses her breath before she regains control of her breathing, and then a giant gasp flies out of her open mouth. The length of the silence always matches the intensity of her orgasm, and this one is a long one, which he didn't expect would happen in the store.

She leans her head back against his bicep and opens her lovely almond-shaped eyes. A huge grin spreads across her face. "Wow," she says softly.

"Wow is right."

She draws in a deep breath. "I lost, but you lose." Her grin deepens.

He chuckles softly as he continues to completely support her body weight. "You are right. And that means I'm making dinner and you are resting on the couch with a glass of wine."

They stand still, her in his arms as others shuffle around them. They stay together for too long, but the awkwardness doesn't register.

"You and me, always, and forever." He kisses the top of her head, then her forehead.

They'd certainly be fucking right now if they weren't in the middle of a grocery store.

"Okay. I accept your penance. But I guess, since I lost, maybe we call this round a wash with you making dinner."

"Deal," he says as he releases her.

"Whew." She lets out a big sigh. "Now, let's finish shopping and go home."

They meander to the meat section and purchase the shrimp and crab cakes from the deli counter. They cruise through the spices aisle to pick up the Italian seasoning and olive oil.

Brad loves the dreamy sleepy look on her face, the euphoria of the orgasm has surely saturated her body.

"How do you feel, babe?"

"I feel wonderful. Incredible." She smiles like she's on cloud nine.

He snickers as they pass the cheese section again. "Do we need parmesan cheese?"

She scoffs. "No more cheese. Let's get out of here."

After checking out, then visiting the liquor store at the exit for two bottles of wine, both white, they head out to their car in the parking lot. The cold air whips at their bodies as they rush along.

"Now that was an unforgettable shopping trip," she says with a giant shudder from the brutally cold wind.

He nods as he hands her the shopping bag. "This whole day will be unforgettable, babe."

She places the bag in the back net of their SUV, smiling at herself despite her embarrassing loss of control in the store. The funny thing is, she hadn't been embarrassed by it at all. The moment Brad caught her in a bear hug, the fear of others watching left her. Her face had been cradled to him so it's likely no one else saw her expressions. However, in truth, the idea of being watched, charging full blast into an orgasm, most definitely turns her on, but the reality of it happening struck a deeper chord of fear in her than she had expected. Regardless, the whole experience had been delicious.

She situates herself in the passenger seat. With an evil grin, she removes her shirt, but holds it crumpled against her breasts.

He enters the car and groans. "Oh, you are really killing me."

"Hey, you just made me come in a grocery store, this is nothing."

"Well, it ain't nothing. Talk to my dick!" He moves in his seat all jittery-like.

She bats her eyes at him. "Whatever do you mean?" she asks in mock innocence.

He starts up the car, trying like hell to ignore her topless next to him. "You are just being cruel now."

"Me?" She gasps. "Oh, hardly."

As they pass by the gas station, Anna yells, "Stop!"

Brad jerks back, alarmed by the urgency in her voice. He glances her way. "What? Did you forget your purse in the store or something?"

"No." She presses her lips together. "We need a car wash."

He peeks at her aghast. "What? In this cold weather?" He pauses and returns his eyes to the road before glancing back at her again. "Now?"

"Yep. Now. And our rules are now debunked because we both lost, and we need new ones." She drops her shirt to fully bare her breasts. "Because our next challenge is going to be in the car wash."

He bursts into riotous laughter. "Damn woman, do you know how much I love you?"

She nods while grinning. "Why yes, Brad. Yes, I do. Now get our asses to that gas station so we can begin our next sex challenge."

He makes a U-turn and takes the car towards the gas station parking lot. He parks with a giant grin, continually glancing at his wife molesting her breasts and nipples. His erection twitches in his pants. His lust is beyond blue balls worthy.

"Okay. Babe. We need a moment to plan. And you are the best wife in the world."

Book 3
The Car Sex Challenge
Chapter 1

They sit in silence for a few minutes, watching the cars coming and going constantly from the busy gas station. Anna shivers as she watches the people shivering as they get gas. Maybe it's being topless, but the heat from the vehicle heater is not keeping her from shaking. The constant motion of people and cars around them is almost dizzying. She feels like a dog watching squirrels frolic.

Of all the nasty places to have a sexual interaction, a gas station? But Anna is proud of her raunchiness pointing them in the direction of the car wash. She's actually giddy with excited anticipation, which spills out of her as a hearty giggle. The strong orgasm from earlier has maybe left her brain a little dopamine-drunk. She's also delighted that the shame of her past relationship ... which she knows she'd experience with him if she ever suggested such a thing as a car wash sex game ... is not plaguing her. She feels empowered and liberated. And hot as absolute fuck. Brad's rehab of her is ever more becoming successful, much to her delight. And no doubt his.

Their eyes meet and the lust in them both swells.

Again, Brad reaffirms for the five-thousandth time how happy he is he asked Anna to marry him. She had been quite reluctant at first. Her first marriage ending had left her wanting companionship, but not exactly desiring to walk back into a married way of life.

"It's perfect! It's private, timed, and no one will know we are playing with ourselves because, essentially, we will be in a tunnel." Anna snickers as she watches a car emerge from the car wash, steam billowing out into the cold winter air like the fattest ghostly caterpillars.

"True. Can I just say again how much I love you and how you think?"

"Yes. Say it as many times as you want. I can't get enough of it." She returns his grin. It's so nice to be appreciated by a man. The twinkle in his eyes tickles Anna. She loves that he loves how her brain works. "And I love that you do." He has always built her up, ever since that first day they met in the bookstore many, many months ago. It was like he didn't know how to tear her down. She's more used to compliments that were laced with negativity, or worse, with no genuine emotion, rare and far between that they were.

"We need rules here. Obviously, it's timed, so we will have that working in our favor. No one has to count or keep track of time. And. No cheating is possible." Brad shifts in his seat as he glances around the gas station parking lot for the umpteenth time. His Dom mode wants to take over this endeavor, but he shushes his inner lead, deferring to her. This was her idea to grace the gas station with their exhibitionist hijinks after all. He rather enjoys giving her these sexually artistic freedoms, when she feels driven by them, just to see where her brain goes. But damn, does he love to lead her in the bedroom. They click so well together, Brad is convinced they were made for each other.

"Right. I think the loser is the one who comes before the car is fully out of the car wash. No car butt in the building, in other words." She snickers and the twinkles in her eyes flare.

"Okay. I'll agree with that." He chuckles at her use of 'car butt'. He taps his finger on his forehead and tries to keep his eyes off of her pert nipples. Even a glance at her with them visible sets his erection thickening. Hell, he constantly thinks of them even when they are covered, let alone when they are visible. A tit slave is what he is, and he knows it.

"Okay. Excellent." Anna's expression grows haughty. "I'll give you a reprieve from my mandate, just while we are in the car wash you can touch my tits."

His eyes light up. "I can? Oh, fuck yes." He rubs his hands together and makes the mistake of letting his eyes drift down to her hardened nipples. His cock thickens, as does his desire to touch her. All he wants to do is drag her to the back of the car and fuck her silly. But he's not giving up this game. And really, he can't. He invented their Day of Play so he'd better finish it, or he will definitely be the big loser. That he would never live down.

Anna narrows her eyes, then raises an eyebrow. "I'm winning this round. Mark my word, bucko." He had fallen in love with her sass and fire immediately back in the beginning of their relationship, especially when she aimed it at him. He loves her strength and zest.

"Bucko?" he asks, aghast but chuckling. "Why am I a bucko now?"

"Hey, bucko, you are a bucko." She nods emphatically with a tiny grin. "Fresh slate for this round though."

"How is that comment a fresh slate?" He gives her a look of mock pouting.

"I'm freshly going to win. Now," she says as she fingers her right nipple, "we first play with ourselves, and that includes while we are in line waiting for our turn, then halfway through the car wash, touching each other is fair game. Whoever comes while we are still inside the car wash loses."

He laughs heartily at her seriousness about something that is clearly frivolous as fuck. "Okay, so, playing devil's advocate, if one of us comes once the car butt is out of the car wash, that doesn't count?"

She purses her lips and moves them all around. "Yes. Right. Exactly." Secretly, she knows she will win. Brad has done enough orgasm permission control with her that she's a pro at holding off. But then again, she had lost it in the grocery store. And he edges himself constantly, pretty much on a daily basis to get her to climax first. Okay. Maybe it's an even match. "Yup. That won't count as being a loser."

"Never thought I'd agree that orgasming meant loser." He screws his face into a silly expression.

She laughs along. "I know, right?" After her fit of laughter slows, she says, "This is rather a backward game."

"It's a challenge more than a game." He points a finger in the air like he's making an invisible tally mark.

"True. That's accurate." She needs an advantage. He hasn't come all day. Technically, that should be her advantage. Ugh. He needs to come. It's always been her coming. Granted, she can have multiple orgasms in a day, but he has been known to have two or three, so he's up for one round at least.

She grabs for his coat in the back seat and slips it on. "I'd better pee before this round. All that water hitting the car might make me spill golden showers down the seat. I don't feel like cleaning up a mess like that!" She's no dummy, and her full bladder will likely cause her to fail because she will have less resolve with all the sexual stimulation. She slips out of the car in a rush. A bit impulsive venturing out without a shirt, but that makes her grin big. She runs along the parking lot, cringing at the cold wind biting at her bare face and hands. It whips her hair in front of her eyes, and she swipes it away as she shivers.

"Fuck, this winter sucks. Why do we live here again?" she mutters as she zips along toward the building.

Brad watches his wife zoom across the parking lot, grinning, loving the fact that she's going in public without a shirt and his jacket is rubbing her hard nipples as she scoots along. She's such a wonderful adventurer and a perfect match for his sexual longings too. A match made in a bookstore. He didn't believe in lightning strikes, but it had to have been kismet that they met that day. He'd never thought he'd find love again, and one so deep and perfect. He hated the word 'perfect,' but it felt right. They are perfect for each other. He'd often wondered if God made people for each other, and before Anna, he'd have scoffed and called the preacher of that nonsense bogus. But it's something he knows deep in the thickest parts of his heart.

He glances at his phone, wondering if one of his kids would be sending a text. Well, he hoped they would, but nothing. He hadn't heard from them in a while. It's definitely time. He loved his kids more than life itself, and seeing them grow up and become responsible, mature men had been important, and a gift. He always wanted to be a good example for them. Now, with Anna, he's modeling a good husband for them. That is extremely important to him to leave such a legacy with his boys. Bless Anna for allowing it to happen.

After a few minutes, Anna bursts from the front door in a flurry of hair flying up as the wind whips her body relentlessly. He smiles. He loves her hair. He could spend hours running his hands through it, which was ideal because all the lush hair follicles on her head combined were one of her erogenous zones. He had learned that one day when he had grabbed her hair into a ponytail as he had railed her doggystyle from behind. The act of him controlling her with her hair as he rammed his dick into her had made her climax in less than a minute. Now he used it on her as a power move. He loved figuring out her triggers and then exploiting them to her benefit, because he benefitted too, because getting her off as much as possible was one of his strongest, if not the strongest, of his kinks.

She yanks the door open and slides inside in a rush. "Well, that'll put a permanent chill on the clit."

"Oh no, we can't have that!" Brad says beguilingly. "And that gives you an advantage. Maybe I need to step out for a moment and freeze my balls off, so our playing field is even here." He reaches for the door handle as he holds her gaze.

She shoots him a look of mock surprise. "Go for it. It's not pleasant out there by anyone's standards. But I get wanting the advantage of cold shrunken balls for this." She chuckles heartily, not surpassing her delight at her own comment at all.

He pops open the door and the wind barrages him with a frigid arctic blast. "Oh damn," he exclaims, but forges out into the cold gusts anyway. He shudders, missing his jacket. The thought of her nipples being cupped by his jacket did nothing to help cool his lust, though.

He slides back into the car.

"Didn't work, did it?" she says with a witchy cackle.

He sighs and screws his face into a dissatisfied smirk. "Nope, not a bit. I keep thinking about my jacket rubbing your bare tits and I'm lost to it."

"Oh, I know the power my boobs have over you." She moves her hands around like she's doing a witch's spell.

"And don't even get me started on that clit of yours."

She smiles with deep satisfaction. "It's got ninja moves." A man who does things out of a need to savor and pleasure her is so much better of a life. She cringes thinking of an old relationship where he just did things just to do them. Sort of like ... checkbox sex. Brad is a savorer, a cherisher, and a wonderful indulger, both to her whims and his own. He spoils her, which builds up their whole relationship. Right from the start, she ate up his passion like a juicy watermelon on a hot summer day. It soaked into all of her and left her craving every wet speck more he had to offer. Her thirst for them together had always been insatiable. Their sex life had been juicy from the very start and only had gotten plusher and more generous, and deliciously controlled. She had never expected she'd enjoy being controlled in the bedroom, but everything Brad had done had brought them naturally to the level of power exchange they enjoyed.

She looks distracted.

"Are we ready for this show to start?" he asks as he turns up the heat.

She flings open his jacket, baring her breasts for his ogling eyes, and tosses it in the backseat. "I'm ready to do this popcorn stand."

"It's a popcorn stand?"

"Mind your own business, bucko." She raises her hand. "Wait! I see a folly in our plan."

"Oh? How so?" Brad turns to his wife, but his eyes fall to her naked chest.

She smiles salaciously as she watches his eyes drop. She loves her power over him, and she intends to use the fuck out of it today. "What if we aren't trying hard enough when we are playing with ourselves? It will give the other an advantage if one of us takes it easy."

Brad nods slowly. "Hmm, I see your point. We need a control on lackluster masturbating. That's a form of cheating here." He thinks for a moment. "How about we make a pact to try our hardest to make ourselves come? Then we will be on an even playing field."

"Okay. And we have to swear we will do it, and not lie." Her eyes go wide as she turns serious.

"Right. Agreed." He snickers. "Beat off hard. Or else." He laughs as he backs up the car and drives his topless horny wife over to the car wash. As they pass a man walking toward the gas pump from the gas station, he smiles wide and gives them a salute.

Brad and Anna's eyes meet with a knowing look as they chuckle.

"Gave him a show," Anna says sweetly.

"Just you naked is a show," he says very matter of fact.

"Aww," she coos as she tips her head to her raised right shoulder. "You say the nicest things, B."

They approach the car wash kiosk and Brad reads the car wash menu. He turns to Anna. "Babe, you realize we have food that needs to be kept cold and we're taking a detour into a hot, steamy building, right?"

She screws her face up into a pained look. "Oh, good point. Oops. Well, we can just do this once or something, and then head home. We are already in line with someone behind us. So, we have to go through now."

"Yup. We're trapped." He chooses the longest wash and closes his window. "Dang, that's a cold wind."

"Freezing off your nuts?" she teases as she plays with her nipples.

He can't take his eyes off of her touching them. His lust is ferociously raging up with each passing grab and caress she does of her nipples. "I'm practically drooling over here. And ... you said nuts," he says with a lascivious grin. They had made a playful deal one day. If she ever says 'nuts', she has to touch his balls. Hell, she doesn't mind. She loves getting him going.

She bites her lip. "I ran right into that one, didn't I?" She jerks her head back sharply. "Me first."

"Always," he says.

She slyly reaches between her legs with a blaze of mischievous lust in her eyes. She does one exaggerated squeeze of her mound, then reaches for his cock, slides her hand down to cradle his balls.

"You did that on purpose, didn't you?" he says with a sigh as she fondles his balls. "Mmm fuck."

"No, but I'll take credit for that anyway." She gently massages and squeezes his balls as he groans.

"Oh, this is a bad start for me." His head lolls back and forth across the headrest of the seat, his eyes rolling back. "I wonder if we are on camera right now. The attendant is going to get a little porn show at work."

"Well, I'm glad you said that because that's hot as fuck." She grins. "We can be his entertainment."

Their eyes meet and the fire in them rages higher.

"I'm game to go forward with this. You?" he asks between pants. The little grin on his face grows more lecherous by the second.

"Oh, I'm full in." She cups his balls and swipes her hand up his hardened cock. "Oops, detour." She smirks and laughs. "Roadwork is a bitch, ain't it?" She wrinkles her nose and a saucy gleam of flirtation sparkles in her eyes.

He smiles through his pleasure and gasps. "I might lose before we get into the car wash what with you touching me and you playing with your nipples like this." His speech is breathless and strained.

"Good. It's your damn turn, bucko!"

The garage door to the car wash opens and steam billows out. So much steam that they can't even see the car ahead of them.

"Onward," Brad says with a nod as he straightens in his seat.

"Onward," Anna agrees while still messing with his privates.

She releases his cock and settles into her own seat, being a good girl now keeping her hands to herself to follow their agreed-upon rules.

"After this round, I need a sandwich," Anna declares.

"Ditto," Brad says. He could likely eat three.

Brad maneuvers the car into position inside the car wash based on what the lit sign prompts tell him to do. The car raises slightly as he gets into position on the little ramp. The stop sign notification lights up and he puts the car in park.

Anna's heart races in anticipation.

"Okay. Go," Brad commands.

He slips his hand inside his pants and begins to stroke his cock just as Anna slides her hand inside hers. They maintain eye contact as they touch themselves, which is erotic entirely on its own.

They'd dabbled in mutual masturbation a bit, which just drives him wild every time. He gets insanely high, like it's a drug high to see Anna pleasuring herself. He always ends up getting hot and, much to his chagrin, even jealous because he wants to be the one giving her the pleasure, yet he still loves the whole act of mutual play. His favorite part is when she looks helpless and a bit shocked or even scared before she orgasms. There is nothing more delicious to him than watching her go into that uncontrolled vulnerable state, then splash into convulsions as she comes. It's just beautiful to watch. He's most certainly addicted to it, if there is such a thing. Likely there's not, and if someone ever called him a freak for it, he wouldn't give a fuck anyways. It's one of life's greatest pleasures to watch your woman orgasm and he's fortunate enough to have a woman like Anna who adores him and all his passion. Anna is a gift in so many ways.

They had both realized early on that what they had was special, and like no other relationship either of them had ever had before, or ever would again. He recognizes he's lucky every day and he shows her it every moment he can. Life is short, especially with the ones he loves. Too short. He'd learned that if he didn't seize the moment, he might never see that feeling again, and he desperately didn't want that with Anna. Even a moment lost, a missed opportunity to please her, is a tragedy.

Anna watches Brad stroke his cock with greedy eyes. It's so yummy to observe his face contorting into a myriad of joy and want. It's a kaleidoscope of lust and pleasure. It's so satisfying and makes her clit twitch when he teases her, especially when he's about to come. He has some kind of sexual magic over her, which she knows only came from building trust, then their intimacy. She'd lacked both in her previous marriage, so she clung to it with Brad like gold, or even oxygen.

"When do I get that cum?" she asks breathlessly.

"Not yet, you don't." His words are clipped short, he can barely verbalize. He's in real danger of losing this round. Spreading his precum all over his cock makes him wish Anna at least had a shirt on because just looking at her body half bare is sending him into overdrive.

"You sure about that? You look pretty ready to blow. Ripe as a stretched water balloon on a faucet," she whispers in a seductive, suggestive tone. She slips off her pants to mid-thigh so he can see her pussy mound. She slips her hand between her legs and begins to finger her clit gently, then vigorously, which sets her moans on an escalation path.

He groans deeply along with her sounds, wishing like hell it was his fingers plunging between her lower lips.

She pulls her wet fingers from her slit and spreads her fingers apart. The string of juices between her fingers reminds Brad of how she tastes, and damn, does he want to swipe his tongue over her fingers to clean them off. She shoves the fingers in her mouth and moans. Her eyes are lit up with teasing. "Mmmm," she coos. "Bet you want a taste."

"Well, that's not helping my cause." He gasps, then snorts. "I'm fucked."

She continues to aggressively play with her pussy, unleashing her persuasive influence over his resolve to not climax.

"Yes," she mutters.

Quite frankly, he's a goner. He's most definitely nearing the edge of his climb. He gasps deeply again, then groans. The rise of pressure building inside him is almost unstoppable at this point.

Just when he's about to lose control, a horn blares from outside the car wash. He stops stroking himself momentarily to look around. It's just what he needs to simmer down.

"Whew," he whispers.

"Hey, who said you get to stop?" she demands with a cross look.

He grins, knowing he's been caught. "I'm still touching." That's true. His hand had not left his cock.

Her expression grows angrier. She can't argue with that. Damnit! She had almost had him spewing. She had almost won. Damn car horn.

The middle sign lights up on the instructional unit of the car wash signaling the next stage of the car wash is underway.

"Ah! We're halfway," Anna exclaims with glee. Since she's already climaxed in the grocery store, she's not as horny as he is, so this is her big chance to win this round. She scrambles to get on her knees facing him and leans forward, making her tits fall, a position she knows drives him bonkers with raging desire. She lowers her top half down to hover over his cock with a muffled chuckle.

He shakes his head. "Oh, no. Fuck. I'm screwed."

She consumes his cock head inside her hot, moist mouth. He groans so loud that his yell rings out louder than the car water spray blasting the windows. He thinks of annoying things, like this employee at work who constantly wastes company time, and his neighbor who sticks his nose in everyone's business and even Brad's garbage bin. The more annoying thoughts the better. He watches her tits swing as she bobs her head on his cock and he rages into the brink of coming.

"Ah, fucckkkk," he says it all drawn out.

He slams his eyes shut so he doesn't get the overpowering stimulus of watching her give him head. Edging is fun until it's not. He slams his hands into the steering wheel three times, then grips it hard. Don't come, don't come, don't come, he screams inside his mind.

An alarm chirps and he opens his eyes. It's telling him to drive forward. "Gotta drive, babe." He lets out a slow, low whistle as she sits up. Saved by an alarm.

She presses her lips together firmly. "Oh pooh." She settles in her seat. "Damn. I almost had you." She looks so disappointed, he almost wishes he had let himself come. She didn't need to stop, not technically, but he's not going to alert her to that.

"Now I have to start all over getting you to the edge," she says in a huff. Good thing she likes doing that.

"Well, I wouldn't say you need to start all over. I'm pretty cocked still, babe."

Her expression is pissy, but her eyes are telling a story of the flirtatious nature of her heart.

He's the luckiest man in the world.

She leans against the door and opens her legs, draping one over the seat and putting the other on the dash. Her pink pussy is moist.

He catches a whiff of her lush feminine scent and visibly swoons.

"Well, shit. Will you look at that?" His eyes scan her wet hole hungrily. She's inviting him into her private world right when he can't visit it. His heart races as he imagines slurping his tongue right up her slit and massaging her clit with rapid circles.

As Brad moves the car forward, Anna plays with herself.

The huge dryers start up with their roars of blasted heat. Brad's cock throbs, ready to spew. He inches the car along slowly, which takes a big effort to control with how far he's on the edge of orgasm.

Anna moves so fast that she seems like a cartoon character. She flies at him at record speed and has his cockhead in her mouth before Brad even takes his next breath.

"Oh, shit, fuck me!" Brad yells as he lifts his foot off the brake so the vehicle lurks forward faster.

Anna garbles some words, but with her mouth full of cock it comes off as gibberish.

Brad laughs, which is a great reprieve from being on the cusp of climax. He presses the accelerator so they move forward way faster than the dryers can work. He doesn't care. Let the wetness freeze the doors shut. They'd melt quickly in their heated garage if they froze anyway.

The car charges out amid blasts of steam as they exit the car wash.

Anna makes an annoyed dissatisfied grunt and pops her mouth off his cock.

"What was that, love?" Brad asks in a teasing tone.

"That was cheating," Anna says as she wipes the corner of her mouth with her hand. "You rushed right through the heater phase." She sits back in her chair with her lower lip out in a pout. She crosses her arms over her breasts.

And it's just in time. The gas station attendant is standing at their door.

Brad pulls up his pants over his cock quickly, then glances at Anna, who is completely buck naked in the front seat.

She widens her eyes in a desperate look of shock and dives to the back seat for cover. She scrambles to get under Brad's coat.

The attendant's grin is so wide, his eyes knowing.

Brad rolls down the window.

"Hello, good sir," Brad says with a beaming grin.

The attendant is a man likely in his forties with hair to his shoulders, and a jacket that looks like it's meant for someone living in Alaska with its thick fur-trimmed hood.

He clears his throat. "Sorry for the malfunction, sir. You can get your money back or go through again."

The gas station worker shifts slightly from foot to foot. If Anna weren't a bit of an exhibitionist, she'd be offended at him trying to peer into the back of the vehicle at her. Instead, she smiles and considers ditching Brad's jacket since he's clearly not offended by what they just did.

Brad's expression goes quizzical. "Malfunction?"

The attendant chuckles heartily. "Yeah, you didn't notice it skipped two levels of the service?"

"Uh. No, I guess I didn't." Brad is dumbfounded. He has zero clue what this man is talking about.

Anna scoffs loudly in the backseat. "Seriously? That's so not fair."

Brad busts a gut. He made it through this round due to a machine malfunction. The stars are aligned for him today.

"This requires a re-do," Anna says with an exasperated sigh. She lets the jacket fall and her breasts bounce into view.

The attendant grins deeper. "Do you want to go through again? It's free." His expression is beyond eager.

Anna smirks. He just wants to watch them. She wonders if he set it to malfunction on purpose.

"Nope, we're good." Brad nods, pretends to glance around. "Looks like we are good and clean. We've got groceries to get home. But thanks anyway."

"Alright, good day to you. And have fun." The attendant backs away still grinning like he won the lottery.

"Well, fuck. That's just piss poor luck for me." She crawls to the front seat as Brad pulls out into the gas station parking lot. Anna turns up the heat. "I'm cold now."

"So, get dressed," Brad says like it's an obvious solution, but his tone is teasing.

"No," she says with determination.

He bites back his laugh. "Let's get these groceries home, babe."

Chapter 2

"How did I possibly lose this round? I had you right where I wanted you. I totally had you in the palm of my hand. You were about to lose, admit it." She shoots him a piercing look.

"Yes, you are right. I almost lost it several times. And I believe you had me in the roof of your mouth, not your palm."

Her cheeks blush. Her anger boils. "Total bs."

Her sitting in the seat next to him naked makes him hornier. All he wants to do is drive to a side street and rail her pussy on repeat until she creams on his cock in orgasmic convulsions as he paints her insides with his cum.

She makes a sour face.

He smirks openly because even when crabby she's hot. He's tempted to say it.

"I have plans, you know."

"Good. I like it when you have plans. So does my cock." He maneuvers the vehicle around oncoming cars.

She settles into the seat and adjusts the vents blasting heat her way. "I'm not sharing."

He chuckles as he drives. There are times in his marriage when he couldn't adore his wife more and this is one of them. He especially adores the fact that she wants to make him come. His last relationship before he met Anna had started like a volcano and died a quick smothering death when she had clung so hard to his every move that he couldn't breathe. Miranda was the neediest woman he'd ever met. And judgmental as she was green with jealousy. He couldn't even talk to another woman, even for work, without her inquisitions plaguing his every move. Every picnic, every bar, every church event if he was chatting with a woman, she had made a beeline for them and butted herself into the conversation. Six months and it was done and over like old chicken in the freezer. Just plain garbage. So, Anna had been a fresh breath of air. She was confident in who she was and did what she did because she wanted to do it. It wasn't about pleasing him, yet what she did pleased him. It was the perfect combination. He had always loved confident women. Women who knew themselves and didn't apologize for living their lives the way they wanted. She had been admirable from the start.

"I've got the perfect line of attack." Her eyes narrow into slits. She rubs her hands together.

He laughs. "Being attacked by you is one of my top joys in life, Anna."

She tries to not grin but fails. "Tread careful, ninja."

He laughs at that harder than the last comment. "Oh, now I'm the ninja. Nice." He nods.

"Ninja at escaping climax. Yeah. But I'm the ninja samurai."

"I don't doubt that for a second, my love." He holds her gaze for a moment. "Bring it, baby."

Anna eyes up Brad. She knows really that he's the one in charge in the bedroom, which she adores. But she also knows that she calls all the shots. She had come to think of Brad as a pleasure Dom. One who was dominant but not into harsh stuff that the media often portrays Dom's as wanting. He was a Dom that didn't crave the sadistic stuff. Being a dominant and submissive wasn't something either of them had ever discussed, yet the description seemed to fit him and her to absoluteness. Yet there were times she flourished as an instigator, but she always sank into his sexual direction like she'd sink into a warm bubble bath. It was luxurious to be loved and fucked by him, which stirred feelings in her she never imagined were possible. There were times he'd just send her a look and she knew exactly what he was thinking, which he always deliciously proved with his next move.

They just understood each other. She'd never been in this situation before where her lover knew her better than anyone on Earth, and not only did he not run away, he celebrated her down to her little toenails. It was a blessing beyond her wildest dreams that she had met Brad.

She sighs heavily. "Well, I guess that was a tie then." Her eyes twitch and her expression reveals she's thinking something she might blurt out.

He reaches over and swipes his fingers around her erect nipple, savoring all her bumps and wrinkles gathered on her areola.

"I should pull over and pay attention to both your nipples at once." His voice is low and sexy.

She sighs as she rolls her body against his caresses. "Mmmm. That feels amazing." She wants nothing more than for him to do just that.

Anna's phone buzzes. She grabs for it, but Brad keeps molesting her nipple.

She reads the text with a frown, so Brad pulls his hand away. He's smart enough to read her and now is not the time for nipple play with that look on her face.

After a full minute of silence, Brad asks, "All okay, babe?"

She sighs and shakes her head. "Not really."

"Oh?" he asks, his voice swollen with concern.

"She just doesn't know when to stop and let things be."

Brad nods, instantly knowing exactly who texted. "She's still harping on that, huh?"

"Afraid so. I wish I had never even said anything about it. She just doesn't accept my answer. She keeps pressing. It's like does she really want me to be coerced? Why wouldn't you want it to be natural?"

"Yeah, that makes no sense. If you are going to share something, I want it to be because you want to share something. Not because I obligate you to."

"Exactly. It's like she's entitled to the information' because she's my sister." She lets out a huge puff of air.

"Relationships don't work that way. Not healthy ones anyway."

"Nope."

This is something Anna had learned as she had matured. Many of her relationships earlier in her life had left her feeling obligated to them, rather than living in her true feelings. It was not a healthy way to live, and she had been enabled into that way of thinking, that ill way of life, and it had all started with her mom, then her sister had followed. She understood it all now. Good standing in relationships should be earned, not expected. And that earning should never stop. Brad had taught her that and it really made sense to her. It had been very freeing on the one hand, but her sister was not following suit, no matter how hard she tried to get her to see that. In her sister's mind, her life, mind, and heart, were all free game to her, owed. And that was based more on the past than the present. Anna had realized she owed her sister nothing and if they weren't on good terms, she didn't owe her any explanations either. It was her secret to share, or not share, and she had the right to say 'no'. Just as every human on the planet has the right to say 'no', so did she. And that was okay. If her sister couldn't accept that, all the more reason to not share deep intimate things with her. She'd keep her behind a wall and unfortunately, her sister would never get that.

"It's hopeless." She sighs. "I just need to let it go."

"How can I help?" he asks kindly.

"You do help. By orienting me in healthy thinking, and by being my sounding board so I don't fall back into enabler mode." She smiles at Brad. "I can't believe how much you've helped me grow and become confident."

"Well, you were well on your way before me."

"I know. But I'm serious, I wouldn't be where I am without you. You're my rock."

It is time for a sex joke.

"Oh, I'm your rock alright. I have a rock-hard cock in my pants with your name all over it."

She snickers and the smile lingers. Her eyes light up. "Well-placed joke, my love." She reaches over and gives his erect cock a squeeze through his pants. "I happen to love rocks."

"Oh, you can do that anytime you want." He grins as he pulls into the driveway.

"Good talk," she says with a nod as she pulls her hand away.

"Aw shit! What is this?" Brad exclaims with disgust.

"What?"

"The car is overheating. The notification just came up. What the hell?"

"Well, good timing," Anna pipes up. "At least we're home and aren't stranded on the side of the road in this cold weather." She sits up straight. "Imagine if we had pulled over to fuck and the car had died there?"

His expression flits to a comical one as he says, "Yeah, with you being naked and all. But we totally should have done that. Car be damned." Then his frown returns. "But, what could this be? We have a coolant leak or something?" He maneuvers the vehicle into the garage and shuts the engine off quickly. "Need to get this engine off so it can cool down."

He presses the garage door button to keep the heat in the garage.

"Do we have any extra coolant on hand?" Anna asks. She's impressed she actually remembers to ask this.

"Well, I think so. Remember when this happened to your car? I think I saved the bottle in the garage somewhere. Just makes me worry something is wrong with my car. I don't want to have to take it into the shop this week, I've got enough on my plate." He sighs. "But I will if I have to."

Anna opens the car door, and the warm air from the garage is a blessing. She's so happy he had talked her into heating their garage. It had seemed like such a waste of money, but it really made life so much easier. Getting in and out of the car was so much nicer all winter long now with it being heated. Plus, all the snow and slush melts right off the cars and Brad just squeegees it out. And it's absolutely perfect for being naked in the garage.

She laughs.

He snorts. "How can you laugh right now?"

She giggles again. "I was just thinking about how nice it is that we have a heated garage, and how that works out so well for being naked in the garage."

He roars with laughter. "I fucking love you, you know that?"

She can't wipe the huge smile off her face even if she were to try.

Brad pops the hood and goes around to the front of the vehicle to raise it up. "Let's see what's going on here."

Anna joins him, ignoring the groceries for the moment. She has plans. She leans over into the space between the engine and the hood, and her breasts fall forward.

Brad glances at her and her breasts hanging as she's slightly bent over the engine. The sight makes his erection thicken. The engine light had killed his boner, but it's back in full force. He shifts to get a better view of her and bonks his head on the hood.

"Fuck!" he exclaims. "Ow!" He steps back from the hood with a chuckle. "Your hanging breasts, babe. Fuck. Trying to cop a gander at them."

She guffaws. "Game plan initiated." The seduction in her voice is unmistakable.

"Well, I've all but lost already." He chortles. "Did you magically get my car to flip on that warning light?"

She pops open the little door to the coolant chamber. "Nope. Wasn't me."

"You naked snags me into major boner status. But you naked in the garage, looking at engine things, fuck. I'm a goner. This is hot as fuck. I'm your sex slave. Do with me what you will." He raises his arms and walks backward toward the workbench. "What are our rules now? Or is everything out the window?" His voice comes off a bit desperate as he backs up to the bench, palms still facing out from his body, eyes showing he knows he's a goner.

Anna goes up on her tippy toes and peers bent over into the engine deeper.

"Fuck me," he mutters. "If that ain't a picture worth a thousand-million words, or I ain't a dick owner." He pulls out his camera and takes some pics of her as she giggles. "Straight out of a nudie magazine, babe, and centerfold material." He lets out a low slow whistle as she swivels. "Damn, woman. You trying to stop my heart?"

She nods with a seductive look as she slowly meanders toward him with a deliberately slow swagger. Her breasts sway back and forth like a pendulum as she shifts her hips in a sashaying walk.

Brad knows he's lost this round already. He scrambles for ideas for how to switch things in his favor in this situation, but he's got nothing. He's so turned on he could come in his pants.

"I'm in big trouble, aren't I?"

She nods while giving him a hard and direct fuck-me-eyes look. "You are toast."

"Just don't burn me," he says in mock weakness. He wants every bit of what she's about to dish out.

She drops to her knees in front of him while keeping eye contact with him. She nuzzles her mouth at his zipper and grips the tag of it with her teeth. She drags it down halfway.

He groans out and drops his head back. His hands grasp her head. He tangles his fingers into her lush hair.

She leans her face against his erection through his pants and wiggles her hand along it.

"Fuck fuck fuck fuck me," he whispers through his panting.

"Look ma, no hands," she says in a southern accent. She puts her hands behind her back and pulls the zipper down the rest of the way with her clenched teeth. She bites his pants near the button and attempts to tug his pants down with her mouth.

He laughs. "You are just the best, babe."

It doesn't work so well to get his pants off so he helps shimmy them down a bit so they are down to his mid-thighs. He goes for the elastic of his underwear, but she raises a hand.

"That I can do with my mouth." She raises an eyebrow.

He's all for that happening so he just watches her, waiting for the delicious unveiling of his cock.

She slides her tongue under the elastic of his pants while keeping her eyes on his. She licks all along the edge of the elastic back and forth twice, spending extra time licking his cockhead that is now sticking out the top. She bites the elastic band and yanks down his underwear to allow his erection to swing out.

"Mmmm, and what do we have here?" Still not using her hands, she nuzzles her face all along his shaft. Her skin on his warm taut skin is a luxurious sensation.

He grips the edge of the workbench as she takes his cockhead in her mouth without using her hands. She rides his cockhead up and down, rubbing her tongue along his frenulum.

His mind is lost as he falls into the moment of pleasure. The groceries are forgotten. The car problem is forgotten. All that is occupying his brain is her giving him a blow job naked in the garage. Like this is every man's fantasy and she's giving it to him all her own idea. Well, not entirely true. He had mentioned it once when they were talking about fantasies they'd both harbored for years and not fulfilled. A blow job by a naked woman in the garage is one he had shared with her. Maybe she remembers it. Maybe not. But either way, he doesn't give a fuck. He's just enjoying it.

She brings her hands around and clasps one around his shaft and the other at his balls. She fondles his balls lightly and strokes his shaft with the other as she works his cock over in her hot warm mouth. She sucks harder and strokes more aggressively and he groans out. He leans back against the workbench extra glad for the support. His heart races and he's nearing the edge of his climax. He realizes he's powerless to stop it. It's over. He's lost this round.

She hums with his cock in her mouth and he gasps then groans deeply. He tries to reach for her nipples to take the focus off of himself, but barely grazes them as he fully succumbs to the urge to ejaculate. He can't stop it and he explodes in her mouth. His cock jerks inside her orifice as she keeps humming her pleasure.

"Mmmm. Mmmm. Mmmm."

His body shakes. His heart is pounding. It's a huge orgasm after all this edging all day. This is a sexual encounter he will remember for life. Whereas the others may blend together, this seduction by Anna naked in the garage has cemented in his brain.

"Oh, fuck me, that was huge," he whispers hoarsely with great effort.

She leans back and rests on her knees as she wipes the corner of her mouth. "You are telling me, that was a lot to swallow." She grins. "I wasn't sure I could handle it."

He laughs with delight and staggers over to the recliner. He's very grateful for the soft armchairs they'd added to their finished garage space. He needs help to get off his shaking legs.

"Whew, that was a biggie. I need to sit for a minute." His panting continues.

Anna crawls over to him, tits hanging, and lays her head on his lap. He strokes her hair and gazes down at the top of her head lovingly. "Your plan was a huge success, babe."

"No doubt. High time you lost a round," she coos lightly.

They sit this way for five minutes, him playing with her hair, her breasts nestled against his leg. He had turned up the heat in the garage yesterday with the frigid temps forecasted. And dang was he glad he had because if it were as cold in here as yesterday, she would have been a shivering mess and this whole erotic scene would have never happened. He soaks in the warm afterglow of orgasm and caresses her scalp as he fondles her hair.

"My turn," he whispers in a commanding voice.

"What? What do you mean? This round is over." She looks up at him in surprise.

"Not yet it's not." He gives her a pointed look of seduction. "I have plans."

He reaches down under her armpits and pulls her up to straddle his lap. Having her body pressed to his wakes up his limp cock and it hardens into a semi.

"Oh, really now," she asks as he fondles her breasts.

"I've been dying to get your nipples in my mouth for a long time now." He continues to feel up her breasts as she slips her fingers into his hair.

"Have you now?" she whispers with delight.

"Yes." He's amazed at how they'd kept each other's sexual interest piqued this far into the day. He had thought it was possible if he made it a priority, but honestly, even to his hopes, this day has far exceeded anything he had imagined when he dreamt up this day of play in the first place. And it wasn't anywhere near over. He imagines this day will be better than most people's whole honeymoons by the time it's over. But with their match of sexual drives and interests, they are an ideal couple.

She smiles down at him as he places kisses on the flesh of her boobs. She loves how he is obsessed with her tits. It's a delicious fact of him that makes her feel very desired. This man definitely knows how to make her feel wanted, desired, lusted for. She sighs as he molests her breasts while planting kisses everywhere on the globes of her breasts.

He makes his way down to her right nipple kissing his way along her skin, his hands caressing, cupping, squeezing her naked flesh. He pushes his pelvis upward to press his growing cock into her tummy. He most definitely wants her to know that even though he's come, he still wants more of her.

He opens his mouth wide and consumes as much of her areola as he can, making an 'oohm' sound as he seals his lips around her generous breast. He sucks hard to get her nipple as far back in his throat as he can. He sighs as he feels it stretch with his hard sucking. He suckles hard on her nipple as she moans out her appreciation.

Her head falls back, and he supports her torso with his left hand so she won't fall off his lap. As she recovers and straightens up, he brings his other hand to her free nipple and pinches it between his fingers. He twists it slightly and pulls it.

She groans out as she digs her fingers into his scalp.

"Oh, damn," she whispers in a voice that sounds more like a kitten mewl.

He takes the hard nugget of her nipple between his fingers like a cigarette and squeezes his fingers on repeat in a pulsing motion. He releases his hard suction from the nipple in his mouth and lightly nibbles at her hardened tit.

"Oh, fuck fuck fuck," she titters. "That feels amazing."

He's not done.

He releases her nipple and grasps both of her nipples with the fingers of each hand. He pulls her nipples away from her body over and over again as she moans and grabs at his hair, his scalp, his ears.

He thrusts his now fully hard cock along her belly. Nothing gets him harder than sucking on her nipples, that was undebatable. And he certainly could mess with her nipples longer than she could stave off begging for him to fuck her.

She shudders as he tugs on her hardened tits.

He fully consumes the nipple he hasn't sucked yet. He sucks hard to pull it to the back of his mouth and he sucks tenaciously to the point of he wonders if it hurts her.

Her groans tell him she's getting deep into the orgasmic zone and he's not letting up.

Anna wants desperately to just stand up and let her victory reign for this round, but his intense attention to her nipples feels too damn good. She can't resist allowing his devouring of her breasts. She almost slumps against him and he immediately supports her back while still suckling at her erect nipples.

"Oh, damn. Fuck," she says in an almost inaudible whisper. The waves of passion undulate inside her and she begins the rise to orgasm. He has made her come with nipple stimulation before, but it's just not a very common occurrence. Usually, she needs her clit stimulated aggressively to come.

As if he read her mind, his hand finds her mound. He sneaks his forefinger into her cleft and locates her clitoral head. He rubs it hard and taps it in a spanking motion.

She yells out at the dual stimulation of her clit and nipple. Damnit. She's gonna end up making this round a tie if she doesn't halt this. Not that she's complaining about an orgasm, but she really thought she'd packaged up this round with a neat and tidy win. She smirks. But isn't multiple orgasms the best win of them all?

She gives in to the rise of her orgasm and allows it to take her to those lovely blissful heights as he aggressively rubs her clit. Her body curls toward his torso. Her eyes roll back as her eyelids flutter. The contractions start in her vagina and continue as her body shakes its way through yet another orgasm.

She sighs and moans as her body settles down from the peak of climax.

"Wow," she says in a soft voice. "That was just ... wow."

With both of them now a cummy wet mess, she slumps against his body and they hold each other. They simply breathe. The euphoria is surreal, like they are one being, floating yet stationary on an easy chair.

After a few minutes, their breathing rates return to normal. Anna stirs.

"I suppose we'd better get those groceries in the fridge. They've been out of coldness for quite some time now. I hope they haven't spoiled." The little satisfied smile on her face is worth gold to Brad.

"Ah, I bet they're fine. No different from having food out at a party for a few hours." He grins. "Either way, all the sexual play and orgasms were worth it."

She grins. "True. Good point." She stands up and turns toward the vehicle. "I'll put them away if you want to tend to the car though. I hope you can find the coolant."

"I think I know where it is." He watches her cute butt walk to the vehicle with a giant growing smile on his face. He loves this woman more than he thought he could ever love someone. Their meeting is a gift he will never question nor regret. It was the best day of his life when he met Anna, and the days with her keep getting better and better.

She snags her clothes from the car and stuffs them under her armpit, then goes for the bags in the back.

"Let me help, babe." Brad stands to assist his wife.

It's a natural instinct with him to help and the fantasticness of that is never wasted on Anna, who never had such awesomeness. She had done most things herself.

"No, it isn't much. I bet I can get it in one trip."

"I don't care. I'm helping," he insists.

She grins. Always the gentleman. She grabs two bags and leaves the other two for him. "You just want to walk behind me and watch my butt move."

"Damn straight I do," he says with a deep chuckle.

The air in the house is warmer than the garage, which is a nice comfort for Anna. She had been on the verge of being cold after climaxing. Not that she'd been horribly cold though, but it definitely felt nicer inside their home. They both place the bags on the counter.

Brad pulls Anna into a hug and they kiss before she snuggles into his chest.

"That was epic. What we just did, hits some big fantasies for me." He breathes in the pleasant flowery scent of her hair.

"Yep. Me too."

"And you remembered."

"I did," she says into his chest, savoring the comfort of being in his arms as much as she's savoring the warm inside air. "This whole day idea is genius, you know."

"I'm enjoying it immensely. It's far exceeding what I had expected. Are you enjoying it?" He could stay this way with her forever.

"Oh, totally I am. You have such good ideas."

He beams. His ex could have never said, or even believed such a thing.

"Okay, I'd better get these groceries in the cold fridge."

He steps back from her not wanting to release her body. "Yup. I'll go add the coolant."

As Brad disappears into the garage, Anna smiles. It's a smile that lives as deep inside her as much as it's on her face. She's a lucky woman to have met Brad. She had thought marriage was a thing of her past. It was a road she hadn't wanted to go down again after her nasty divorce. But her marriage had been nastier, so the pain of the divorce had been worth it all. Especially now that she was in an amazing marriage with Brad. He's like a man angel God had sent her to help her grow, become healthy, and enjoy life once again. The blessings of him just never seem to dry up. Just like this magnificent day.

She pulls out all the cold items and places them in the fridge. Then she finds her clothing and dresses, all the while humming happily. The best part of the day is that it's not over. They have so much more to do. They are going to make dinner together. Eat it. Play more and then as a finale, do their ultimate intimate moment by having sex. She shivers with excitement. On pins and needles wondering what else Brad has planned. He's such a romantic and such a horn dog at once. He's quite literally the most perfect man.

Book 4
The Hide and Seek Sex Challenge

Chapter 1

"Will you quit?" Anna flings her hand at Brad and flecks of flour fly off. She wants him to play with her pussy, but now he's just being a pest. "I'm making bread, and if you don't let me finish, it won't have a chance to rise." Despite her annoyed tone, she loves his hyper-focused attention.

He chuckles and joy blooms in his gaze. "Oh. I have a rise for you."

"Really? I could do without that kind of cheese." She tries to squash her smile, but realizes her smirk makes her words hollow.

"I know exactly what you want." He presses his hand to her hips and slides it to her belly while snuggling his swollen meat onto her backside. "Your hands most certainly do have a way with that dough, though." His voice is wrought with teasing.

"Green with jealousy, aren't you?" She loses her resolve and fully smiles.

His words often carry sexual innuendo even when she assumes he has no such clear intent. She snickers. Well, maybe that's making him out to be too innocent, with that salacious look covering his face. Maybe that's just her brain, but she doubts it. He's a man of high sexual drive and his passion has always been so delicious to be bathed in, and he always graciously sends her a waterfall of it. There's no pussyfooting around or game-playing with him, which she loves. No passive-aggressive shit or weak excuses for wooing, like in her first marriage.

She smacks the dough with her clawed fists. She doesn't really care about the bread, not really, but evading his advances in a saucy way always seems to blossom their flirting. Bring it, Brad. It is the egging on, the chase and capture that makes their interactions so alluring. The mood that their mutual cajoling incites rings it all-out to the maximum; the very air is contagious for more. He'd taught her it was a dance. It had brought out her playful side that she'd had in her youth, but that got killed by her passionless marriage in a hurry once the stain of their honeymoon waned. A crystal ball of her husband's impending disinterest would have been very helpful that night before the grand wedding. It was like he had caught her and then stopped trying altogether, complacent to just have her cook his meals, clean his house, and raise the kids. For, like, years. The familiar cliché 'romance is dead' was real world for her.

She snorts, frustrated that her thoughts still drift to that loser, even after all these wonderful months with Brad.

She flutters her eyelids at her handsome husband. He's a man who deserves all her focus. She figures he knows she feigns her annoyance with him because he plays along to entice her, like a dancing bird courts his potential afternoon fling. She is never opposed to being wooed by Brad. It is one of the best things in life, and she'd never discourage his silly romantic plans to seduce her. The whole game, when she fully acquiesced, that's when their sex got really juicy. And honestly, seduction is never silly, on any level. Being starved of it for decades, she knows that only too well. She pushes the thoughts of her lame deadbeat ex out of her head. She's with Brad now and life is proving that choice to be beyond glorious every second of every day. But he certainly could be infuriating too, mostly in a sweet way.

He meanders his fingers down her belly and rests them on her mound.

"Tease," she says as she molests the dough ball into a proper lump to begin its rise.

"Always, and ultimately never," he whispers as he nibbles her ear.

He's not wrong. His follow-through is impeccable.

"Persistence makes for explosiveness."

She squirms in his arms, which brings him to sway the both of them as one. She is ready to spin and kiss him, to open her legs wide for his ever-exploring fingers, but she stays put. It's too exciting to preempt his intentions, she yearns to see what he has in mind. It will no doubt be ripe with desire and aimed at her pleasure, she has no doubts. She isn't into cutting the rosebud off before it blooms fully.

She pries herself from his arms, even though that's where she wants to stay, and goes for the plastic wrap.

He follows her body closely like a magnet, some part of him still touching her even as she walks. Most women might shoot him a look of admonishment, yet she tries to hide her enthusiasm, just for the sake of the conquest.

"I'm going to start calling you cling wrap." She resists the urge to heckle his desperate seeming efforts.

He pulls her fully to him from behind and wraps his arms around her in a hug that might pop her head off it's so strong.

She laughs with delight. "Or Anaconda!"

He growls and fondles her breasts like a hungry bear who got his paws on a bag of candy.

"I have a plan," he announces without releasing his death grip on her.

"You let me go first, then I'll listen." Instantly she wants his body pressed back to hers though, like a wanton teenager whose parents pulled them from the secrecy of her bedroom, just as things had been about to get interesting. And fun.

He obeys and steps back from her. "Okay. If I must."

She covers the metal bowl with the wrap, stretching it to the max as she sideways watches him to see if he's complying. She taps the taut plastic sheath over the bowl and sets it on the warmed stovetop. "Okay, that sits for an hour."

"Perfect," he says with conviction, "just enough time to make you come twenty times."

She drops her jaw and twirls out of his reach.

"Who's the tease now, my elegant gorgeous sexy as fuck ballerina?" His eyes twinkle. He's a toddler ready to burst with indulgent impatience, which in truth delights her to her core and then down to her painted toes. "I have the best plan for our next round, and it involves you wearing something I've been hiding from you."

She raises an eyebrow at him as she tips her head. Oh, he's good at this. "Really now? Do tell." It was just Christmas, and yet he saved this gift?

"Nope. Not yet." His turn to spin away from her.

She reigns in her desire to jump on his back and tackle him to the ground, force him to tell her because that's about the most enticing hook she can imagine. A gift too good for Christmas? Yet saved for an ordinary day in January? Well, today is no ordinary day. A full day of sexual play could never be. She is most certainly intrigued. But she knows she'd never be able to get his secret out of him via her meager feminine strength, because she is but a cat to his brute size and strength. If she's a cat, he's the biggest lion on the prairie. The thought of her trying to muscle him into spilling would make him laugh with delight though. She toys with doing it for a split second. But if she uses her sexual charms ...

Something he's been planning but waiting to spring on her. Her mind reels in anticipation and scheming. It dabs into all the usual areas. Sex toys. Flavored lube. A new technique he'd researched on stimulating the clit. She plants her feet as her panting takes over her calm. Biting her lips together to keep from begging, she busies herself with pulling veggies from the fridge. She must camouflage her greedy excitement.

"I see that want in your eyes, even from the back of your head," he teases with a fortuitous chuckle, which seems more well-planted than spontaneous.

An exasperated sigh escapes her parted lips. Her patience fails her. "One hint?" she begs sweetly without meeting his gaze. She examines the mushrooms she's cutting, waiting with bated breath for even one morsel of the deliciousness he surely has planned.

"One hint, what?"

Her heart races. "Please."

"Please, who?"

Now that she has released a puddle to wet the crotch of her leggings, she knows she's lost this round already. "Daddy."

He moves behind her. He has been saving this move all day, clearly. Him not touching her, but hovering, expertly keeping them only mere inches apart, is more seductive than his actual hands. His lingering is devastatingly enticing, his hot breath on her ear sending a blast of heat right to her pelvis.

A hungry stirring in her lower abdomen pleads for more of his impending passionate domination.

"Good girl."

The words swell her lust like bulbs of grapes he's dangling above her mouth. The urge to bite down on his offering of praise floods her entire body like an avalanche of arousal.

She waits patiently, frozen, not even finishing the pushing down of the knife through the mushroom she'd been slicing.

Thirty seconds pass like an hour before he says in a commanding tone, "It will allow me to guide you without touching you."

She knew it. A new remote control sex toy is the first thing that pops into her head. Her desire salivates inside her gut. She laments never having done this kind of sex surprise for him and makes a mental note to gift him with a toy or piece of lingerie soon. His romancing game is always so good she is constantly spoiled and stimulated at once. Their relationship often seems too good to be her reality. When dreams come true, they don't fizzle like hopes.

"And it's not what you think." He takes a step away without even so much as tapping her.

Her racing heart smacks the inside of her chest as it pumps. Her lips curl. The deep anticipatory gasp stuck in her throat makes it seem that way anyhow.

With his hint rolling around in her brain, she continues to feign indifference as she finishes one mushroom and moves on to the next.

"Care to guess?" He pulls open the fridge and selects a white wine from the door.

"I can wait," she lies. But, in truth, her curiosity is about to bubble out of her eye sockets, it's boiling so heatedly inside her.

He snickers as he unwraps the foil on the top of the bottle. "Care for a glass of white?"

She nods as she moves on to the onions. She is regretting choosing a sauce recipe that requires constant stirring because right now—all she really wants to do is jump on Brad so he falls to the floor so she can devour him, ride him into a monster raging orgasm, or five, and taste the sweet hot nirvana highs of consuming his dick inside her contracting pussy.

"Yes, please." It hurts her to not strike the edging of such a succulent sexual urge.

"You are suddenly awfully quiet." His tone tells her he gets it. "Be a good girl, and remove a piece of clothing for Daddy, and maybe you get another clue."

His use of Daddy in this round is quite effective, she muses as she licks her lips and resists the urge to press her index finger to her begging clitoris.

She hesitates for less than ten seconds before she rips her top off. Her hair flies up as she tears the offensive garment off her head.

He laughs heartily. "Well, that was easy."

She frowns, which helps her to not grin when that's exactly what she desires to do. She throws the shirt at him, and he barely catches it before it topples the wine glasses over.

"If that wild throw is any indication of your mood ... I'm going to enjoy this round immensely."

Brad hands her a very full wine glass and clinks his goblet to hers. "To sex games and orgasms, and your bare skin. I feel a game idea coming on."

Her breath catches as she sips the clear, cool beverage. This is a new idea? The wine slides past her tongue in shades of smooth tanginess, then spreads itself down the back of her throat as she swallows fast. "I'll gladly be your toy for any game."

He raises both eyebrows stupidly in that classically cheesy way, but it only endears him more to her. "That will be arranged." He takes a long pull of his wine as he drags his eyes along her bare flesh. "Each article of clothing you remove gives you another clue, but removing that bra gets you all the way there instantly."

A tease where she gets to decide the rate of seduction. Hmm. This is definitely an intriguing turn of events.

She mulls the options around in her brain—continue to swell his longing or satiate his hunger for her bare tits?

After a minute of silence, Brad clears his throat. "I see this is proving to be a big decision."

She doesn't take the influence of her breasts over him lightly. She intends to enchant him into climaxing this round. Make him come more times today than he ever has in his life. If she fails, at least she will have enjoyed the allurement of trying, as would he, no doubt. He is a sucker for a good hard edging any day.

She needs an innocent question to fish a hint out of him without stripping off another item of clothing. "If I do remove my bra, am I going to be cold?"

He guffaws. "Yes, but I won't let that happen. I'll be ready to envelop you in me or a blanket, that is after I watch your areolas create those tongue-pleasing maps of gathered pink skin first." He fondles her ass with both hands. "Clever girl," he retorts. "You charmed a clue out of me without taking another thing off."

"You don't fool me. You knew before you opened your lips."

"Lips, you say?" He sneaks his index and middle finger to her feminine folds, over her leggings, and massages her pussy through the fabric. "You've kinda wet your leggings, babe."

She writhes against the pressure of his fingers against her hot core as if her pussy were the button that rules her body. At his handling, it is. She twists, trying for more and more of his touch. Damn pants are a damper.

He pulls his fingers away and she pouts, complete with her lower lip protruding past her top.

"But you are making sauce, so let's focus on that. What can I do?"

She holds in her impatience, not letting even the slight puff of a complaint leave her lungs.

She takes the reprieve as a win, but only because she got that clue. Which she realizes isn't as great of a clue as she thought. But she now knows, it is something she is going to wear. Will it be nipple clamps? Will it be lingerie? Will it be crotchless panties? A corset? Her mind spins to toys and designs of sexy clothing they hadn't tried out yet.

She points to the red and green peppers on the counter. "Chop those." Her voice comes out bland and commanding.

He dutifully chops as she prepares the mushrooms for sautéing.

The need to know quickly pickles in her tummy. She is too curious to not find out, so impatient as a youngster with a bowl of cheesy fish crackers held above her head, she grabs for what she wants and quickly unclasps her bra and flings it at his back. It hits him with a thunk, then plops down to the kitchen floor after a fast plummet.

He swivels in lightning speed, grins the most lecherously wicked grin, then speeds on down the hallway towards the stairs. She listens as he trudges up the stairway, seeming like he's stomping his way up so she knows exactly where he is and can follow along from afar.

He reappears faster than she can add the cream to the pan, so she sets the little carton down quickly.

Her heart titters in her chest and doesn't settle down as he hands her a shiny purple box with a large pink bow atop. It's about the size of a box of spaghetti, which makes her believe she will be quite cold wearing this get-up.

Her heart pounds ever harder as she unties the bow. It falls undone slowly and ceremoniously in a grand gesture, just as a proper sex gift bow should. She strings the ribbon around Brad's neck.

"We will use that later." He winks.

"Yes please," she says, her joy at finding out what is in this box mounting higher by the second.

She removes the lid and spreads open the pink tissue paper that had popped up slightly once the lid was off. The contents are clearly too big for this small narrow box as they bounce up now unstrained. A stack of straps attached by metal rings sits inside.

Her eyes widen and her excitement spills out of her mouth as a sigh of delight. "A harness."

"Yes, handmade by a seller online."

She's never worn a harness. Her tits are already hard from being bare, but they tweak a bit more erect as the thoughts flood her brain of Brad grabbing her by these straps during a rough fuck and controlling where her body will go with great ease. Her brain fixates on the idea of him dragging her upstairs by this leather against her skin. Him having his way with her in hours of undulating euphoric positions of sensual inter-and-outer-course, his Dom mode flaring.

"Ah," he says as if it were a sigh. "You like."

She nods as she reaches in to remove the stacked straps from the box. "Help me get into it?"

Her hands shake as she takes the stiff red leather out of the slender box. She salivates as she imagines her body being pulled into doggy with Brad's fingers wrapped tightly around a piece of this outfit, forcing her into a head down, ass up position faster than ever.

"This will be an amazing tool for me to dominate you with."

Her voice stagnates, but she wants to say 'yes' as she savors the look of pure lust and yearning on his face. He loves dominating her as much as she desires it. The yin and the yang of dominance and submission always eggs on their encounters, like how the sun blends into the sky. From where she stands, there is no separation, they are both parts of a bigger picture that she ultimately knows is separate, but feels as if they are one.

Ignoring all the veggies that need to be cut and the sauce that needs compiling, she pushes her leggings down, past her fragrant pussy, over her knees, and then on a slick ride down her shins to off her bare feet. Now naked in front of Brad, who is still fully dressed, she hands him the strappy garment.

"Do the honors?" The thought of him dressing her is sensual and strengthens the feelings she harbors that he owns her. Not like a possession, never like that. Never something to show off like a trophy that never got stroked or taken care of. But as his muse to please fully, explicitly, and completely at all times. His goddess to also fulfill his fantasies in ways she also wants. She had learned she adored him guiding her in the bedroom, and often flat-out telling her what to do. She enjoyed their history of discussions, of debriefings before and after sex, so that he knew exactly what her boundaries were, what her turn-ons were, and she knew his. The best part is that knowing also meant doing, which is also a new concept for her in relationships. She'd grown accustomed to her ex knowing what she wanted, but him withholding doing anything like a cruel master who took joy in depriving his prisoner of any pleasures. Not that he flat-out tied her up and starved her, but a million toothpicks had made a mountain of neglect. The day she left him, she'd torched that mountain and laid siege for the land of Brad. Cheesy thoughts? Yes. But accurate, and blissfully even more of a yes. Back then, she ate cold shoulder most days for breakfast, lunch, and dinner, unless she fit his bill for the day.

The most wonderful thing about Brad was that he'd been very careful to never even tiptoe near her hard 'no' boundaries. If he had a question or wished to discuss a desire of his own, he never pussy-footed around or played games. He just asked, and never tried without first asking. And not feeling any pressure, she simply answered. The natural easy synergy of their honest, mutually respectful relationship defied Anna's brain until one day, it felt real and natural, and not a part of some wish list that was out of her reach. It is her reality and that's when the real freedom set in.

He pulls her to the side, into the open space beyond the island, a deep appreciative expression adorning his loving handsome face. His masculinity is yummy to her as she scans her line of vision from his lips, down his broad shoulders, skimming down his lush tummy, and settling on the grand bulge beneath the zipper of his jeans.

He slowly slips the harness over her head and secures the straps over the sides of her breasts, snugging it to nestle against her skin. He spins her to adjust it on her back before he presses her forward slightly, bending her over in front of him.

"Grab the chair for support," he says as a direct command.

Her pussy wets as he molds her body into position for the pelvic part to ride over her feet and up her thighs. After he secures it to her pelvis, he tugs on the straps framing her ass.

"This will be so fucking perfect for doggy; I can't fucking wait." He yanks on the harness over her hips once more. He bumps her butt from behind in a series of pelvic thrusts, which bounce her body forward on repeat. He continues to hump her from behind, his breathing spinning quickly into panting, mirroring her own ragged breaths.

"Oh yeah," Anna moans.

This doggy dry humping flares her longing for his fat dick up her pussy more than she'd ever remembered it doing before.

"Oh, fuck me," she whispers between pants.

He rams her harder from behind and her vaginal opening widens. After about another ten body slams, he releases the new handle that adorns her lower back above her buttocks and takes a step away.

Her frustration comes out as an impatient grunt. She wants more, desperately so, as if she were suffocating for it. "Please, can I have more of that, Daddy?" she pleads without turning around. She'd save her begging eyes for the moment, in case he denies her the pleasure of more hip pumps against her backside.

"No, babe. Gonna slow down now. I almost came doing that. I'm going to step out on the front step and go get the mail to simmer down. I'm not ruining my plan here. My cock is not entering your pussy until the end of the day, and I'm not deviating from this plan. We've come way too far today to not finish it right."

She laments, but stands and turns to face him, presenting her wanton eyes as her last ditch effort to try to get him to fuck her silly right the fuck now.

"Whew," he mutters as he lurches back from her. "That look is tugging at tearing down my resolve something fierce. I'd better get my ass out of here." He laughs, then dashes out of the kitchen and flies out the front door without a jacket. He comes back a second later, not glancing her way, but stopping only to slip his boots on before scrambling back out the front door.

She sighs. "So close," she mutters.

Her phone buzzes and it's her sister, whom she's not in the mood to tangle with, so she flips her phone over without reading it. Likely, her sister is just harassing her again anyway. She didn't need that downer at the moment, not that she ever needed it, but especially not now when she is on such an aroused hormone high. She'd rather savor her edging without the tarnished spray of her sister's toxicity. Their relationship had grown increasingly toxic, which she had never seen coming, but landed squarely on her in recent years and had not left. Her sister was mad she had gotten a divorce. In her sister's view, Anna had ruined a perfectly good marriage to a perfect man. Even though Anna had told her all the bad shit about her marriage, well, most of it anyway, her sister still disagreed with her decision to leave. She didn't see it because her husband had been very good at hiding it from others. Anna always suspected her sister's anger at her hooking up with Brad was more out of jealousy than anything else. She knew what a selfish ass her brother-in-law could be.

She turns back to her chopping and sauce-making chores with a splurge of wine across her tongue and a fresh influx of joy across her heart. She turns up the music and dances about, twirling and enjoying her own fleshy body parts jiggling as she moves about the kitchen.

"Well, shit, going out in that frigid barren wasteland of our front yard was a total waste. I'm right back where I was with wanting to bend you over and fuck you into oblivion."

She dances her way over to him, bends over when she reaches him and shakes her buns at him. She plucks at the harness straps playfully.

"You wanna, I know it." She laughs at the smack sound he makes, which she figures must be him hitting his forehead with his palm.

"You little minx," he says through heavy breathing.

"Teach me a lesson, then, Daddy," she says in her most seductive, submissive, and mewling tone.

"Fuck. Fuck. Fuck. Fuck. Fuck."

She keeps shaking her ass his way, turning sideways periodically so he can watch her tits swing beneath her body in the same way they move when he fucks her from behind.

"That dick must be awfully lonely," she purrs.

She glances back at him and chortles.

He has his hands over his eyes.

In a strained voice, he musters, "If I can't see you, it helps."

She backs up into him and bumps his groin with her butt.

"Aw, shit," he groans out.

She smacks her ass against him again.

He lays a big hard wallop of a spank across her bottom.

The loud smack of his palm against her flesh is almost as jarring as the sting of the slap itself.

She yelps and flies forward, losing her balance. She squeals and stands up, feeling sheepish, admonished, and embarrassed all at once, which all congeal into some form of inflamed lust she doesn't quite understand, but that is unquestionably real. She reveals her flirtatious chagrin at being treated like a naughty little girl, swiveling to face him and meeting his now uncovered eyes.

"You devil," she charges with a hand on her hip. She can almost cut the lust hanging in the air between them.

"And I'll not hesitate to do it again," he says in mock anger.

"Hmpf," she says before she struts back to her post of duties as head chef. She glances at her backside to see if he made a handprint. "I guess I'd better get cooking or we will be eating that bag of Doritos instead, out of sheer massive hunger." She meets his gaze. "Now, to your peppers, my dear Daddy Dom."

His happy face matches hers as they settle back into boring meal-making tasks, both sipping on wine and humming to the music.

After finishing chopping the peppers, he calls over his shoulder. "I may need you to put your robe on so we actually make this meal."

She grabs a piece of cheese and a hunk of bread and snakes her arms around him from his backside. She has no such intentions of covering up her flesh now.

"Peace offering?" She holds the bread and cheese up.

He bends his head down and takes the morsels from her fingers, licking her fingertips as he does.

"You are asking for another spanking," he says like the devil filled his throat with the slippery words.

"Maybe we just need a snack, make part of the meal, mess around, then come back and finish cooking. I think that sounds like an excellent modification, what do you think?"

He pries himself from her body and turns to face her. He is behind the shield of his hands again.

"Okay, how about this? We make the sauce, with a toy shoved up your pussy, then we take the show to the bedroom for the next phase of my plan. Then, after you come, we will finish dinner and eat it."

She crosses her arms under her pert breasts. "Wait, that all sounds good, but why are you assuming I'm losing already?" she asks, aghast.

"Because you will be losing." He grins big, his mouth spreading wide beneath his hand, which is still covering the top half of his face. "But, with these games, losing is winning. So, really, you win."

"Nice try, bucko." She tugs on the straps that line her sides. "Well, you are coming this round, I'm successfully edging without climax."

"Oh, ye of wishful thinking." His voice is both mocking and lightheartedly jovial.

She knows he's right, but that doesn't mean she's not going to try to make his dick explode too.

"You have to be able to see to edge me, Brad," she says in a dry know-it-all-tone, with a major helping of teasing.

"Nope, I don't, babe." He reaches for his phone, keeping his vision off Anna, and strides into the living room. "Be Daddy's good girl and put the bulb toy in and I'll edge you from the living room with the remote."

The Daddy talk is coming out in full force this round. And she is not afraid to admit that she totally loves it.

She acquiesces and rummages in the kitchen sex toy drawer for the little pink beauty. She locates it and smears the floral-scented lube across its rotund body. Slipping it into her already wet hole is easy, she hadn't even needed the lube. The insertion alone, without fail, makes her groan again, just like it does every dang time.

"Mmm, not complaining at all, but seems this is making the playing ground hysterically unfair."

"Who's in control, babe?"

"You are," she murmurs in a slow drawl.

"You, who?"

He blasts the toy on high, mercilessly. Her body jolts upright, then she sways, undulating to the waves of vibration that are now overcoming her womanhood.

"Oh, fuck."

"Who?"

"Daddy," she mutters in exasperation.

"Good girl," he says soothingly from across the room.

The vibrations flooding her pussy simmer down to the lowest level. "Thank you, I need this so I can be functional." She points her index finger at her abdomen.

He salutes her from the easy chair in the living room. "Yes, my love." He sighs deeply. "But you look so deliciously excited and gorgeous with it on high."

She scoffs. "Okay, I'll buy that. But not when I'm making sauce!" she declares with absolution. "Unless you want burnt sauce, that is."

"I like my sauce hot but not charred, thank you."

"Then behave over there, mister."

"On my scout's honor."

"You aren't a scout."

"Shh, you are ruining my conviction."

She chuckles as she finishes pouring all the sauce ingredients into the pot. She slides all the veggies into the frying pan off the cutting board and stirs them to coat them with olive oil. With two pans ready, but not on heat yet, and the bread rising, they are on their way to a delicious homemade meal.

She turns her attention to compiling the salad as Brad follows the rules and keeps the toy inside her on the lowest setting. Every time she glances his way, he has his attention on his phone or the magazine in his lap. After the salad is nearly as perfect as possible, she bends to place it into the fridge. The toy inside her surges on high and she cries out.

"Brad!" she screams.

"Who?" he demands in a deep, domineering voice.

"Daddy," she corrects.

"Just reminding you that you are all that's on my mind."

She shimmies her shoulders at that yummy confession of his, feeling extra special.

"I saw that sweet little booty wiggle," he calls out, naming her appreciation of his words quite appropriately. "And Daddy likes."

She turns the dials to begin to cook the sauce and veggies. She gasps, realizing she hasn't set the chicken up in the marinade yet. After turning the burners back off, she quickly whips up the marinade and drops the chicken in it, all while Brad runs the toy on a calming, yet still arousing schedule of weak buzzes, jolts, and low-key massaging. She hums along with the song, enjoying a wine-soaked tongue as she returns her attention to the crucial part of the meal, the sauce. Stirring this sauce in constant mode is imperative, so her full attention needs to be on it and nothing else so she doesn't ruin it. The veggies will just have to wait their turn.

"How's it going, babe? Need any help?"

"No, not from a blindfolded man!" she says haughtily. "You will just be in the way."

"Oi, touché," he says in a similar tone back.

She grins as she swirls her spoon through the sauce at a constant rate. She savors him playing with her pussy from afar.

"I still don't think this is very fair," she says in a saucy voice. "How are you even close to coming and I'm half-cocked?"

She waits for the corny sex joke about how that's not true, that she's actually currently cock-less, to fly out of his mouth, but it doesn't come. Instead, Brad ramps up the toy to a higher level.

She struggles to keep stirring the sauce as the toy wreaks luscious havoc on her insides.

"Aw, fuck," she whispers.

"I heard that," he calls her out.

All she can manage is a series of whimpers out of her mouth. He ramps up the toy to the highest vibration and she doubles over, ignoring her sauce.

She winces as the sauce pops on the heat. Those threatening sounds mean it's getting too hot.

"Daddy is enjoying stroking your clit right now. Feel that wave spreading your arousal so high. Yeah, that's my good girl. Come on. Babe, come on. Daddy's yearning to fuck that pussy from behind, pound against your beautiful pussy, your swollen clit. Be Daddy's good girl. Come on babe, that's it. Daddy wants you to come. Come for Daddy, babe. Be my good girl."

She's powerless against his verbal litany. The scrumptious urgency of his voice and added heat of his horny commands flare into an all-out obliteration of her resolve. The offensive, yet mind-blowing, pleasuring toy shows no mercy across her clit and sends her to the very bitty edge of her climax. She moans out, struggling to not climax, then yells as her body doubles over.

The sauce in the pot erupts in a barrage of pops like gunfire, and the harsh smell of burnt cream and cheese floods her nose.

"Ah, shit," she hurls out the words as an outburst, both from the intensity she's enduring from the toy and the apparent demolition of the sauce. "Pineapple!"

Chapter 2

B rad turns off the toy immediately at the utterance of her safe word. She rights her body as she attempts to catch her breath.

"You okay, babe?" he asks, his voice full of concern.

"The ... sauce ... is ... burnt," she gasps out. "Dammit." Burnt sauce also means ruined orgasm. But in truth, she wants it this way. She's determined to win. However, there's no triumph in destroying their dinner.

He hurries over to the kitchen just as she moves the sauce off the heat. The circular burner flares a bright red when the pot is removed.

"Shit shit shit!" Anna blurts. "It's ruined! All ruined! I couldn't stir during that onslaught."

The offensive smell of burnt cheese floods both their nostrils and Anna's heart sinks. She swats Brad's shoulder. She can't help it. She laughs.

"You dolt!" Her laughter boils to a max point. "I can't be a good cook while I'm coming! I can multitask with the best, but not like that."

He pulls her into his arms, laughing, and plants kisses all over her face.

She pouts. "Our dinner is now trashed," she says with a voice full of defeat.

"We will be okay. I'll clean it up, babe. We still have the chicken, the veggies, the bread, and the salad. That's more than plenty for a meal." He rocks her back and forth. "My beautiful wife, you make me smile and delight me every day. Let's ditch this and move on to the next phase of my plan." He knocks his head back towards the stairway that goes up to the second floor. "What do you say, sexy?"

She knows he's right, they will still have a delicious meal without the sauce. "But that sauce is to die for." However, she gives him a look that indicates her interest is piqued. "And that next phase is?"

He chuckles with joy. "Mutual masturbation where each of us must use a sex toy, but the other one gets to pick which one it is. We will see who comes first, and if neither of us comes, we move on to stage two."

"Well, I assure you, I will win. I came earlier so I won't be as ripe as you," she snickers with a little grin.

Not that she doesn't want to come, but she mostly just yearns to hold off so she can find out what stage two is. She releases a titter of giggles as he grabs ahold of her harness. He leads her out of the kitchen and up the stairs to the waiting king bed, pulling her along like a puppy dog. He glances back at her with mischief in his eyes as he tugs her forward. He occasionally jerks his hand, and her body reacts with a lurch. The simple act reminds Anna that Brad is in control, and that's exactly what she loves.

"I've got you so easy now," he slurs. "My pet."

She purrs and meows. "Do tell."

"Come. You need an orgasm appetizer."

As Anna enters the room, she gasps out her surprise. Candles are lit along the walls on every possible surface of their bedroom. The air is scented with lavender with hints of rose. Their sex toys, well at least some of them, are lined up on the padded bench at the end of their bed.

"The arsenal," she states.

"Indeed," he agrees as he releases her harness.

She misses his assertion of dominance immediately.

He strolls over to the standing ice bucket situated by their dresser and pulls out a bottle of unopened champagne. It had been his idea to buy a standing ice bucket for their bedroom and she had laughed at first, but it had proven to be so useful in aiding in their romantic encounters she can't imagine life without one now.

He messes with the cork and wiggles it off. After the usual pop and a puffy mist of champagne spray out the top, Brad pours two glasses for them. He deftly one-handedly handles their wedding champagne flutes they'd had crafted in Hawaii before their small wedding on the beach. After Hawaii, they had flown to Fiji. Her lifelong impossible-seeming dream of sleeping in a hut over the ocean off of a dock in paradise had been realized, but despite the atrocious load of cash they'd spent on their extravagant honeymoon, half of which was spent fucking, the real jackpot was having Brad in real life. And for good because they were now hitched. Happily committed. Which is something she never thought she'd want again, that is until she met Brad. She'd have married him at the justice of the peace, though, in jeans and a tank top, wore a rubber ring from a vending machine for a wedding ring, and honeymooned at the cheapest, scariest motel on the planet. All she had wanted was to be Brad's wife. And she not only has that now, but she is getting to add delectable memories like today to her bank of her and Brad's wonderful new saga. A story she knows is limitless in space and infinite in its ability to hold pleasure. They are the real thing.

"I love this, Brad. When did you have time to do all this?" she asks scanning the room. The flickering candles and aromas scrumptiously adding sensuality to the room, and to her mood. "I was already ready, but wow, this room! It's simply magical!" She shakes her head. How did he sneak up here and have time for all this while she was cooking, and she didn't notice his absence?

He hands her a sex toy. Her new clit sucker.

"Oh, well shit. Now that's not fair at all."

He snickers. "Them's the rules I stated downstairs, you didn't protest, babe. It's all already set."

She snorts. "This toy makes me come in less than a minute when I'm aroused, and I'm sure as fuck aroused!"

"Your point?"

She growls and grabs Brad's fleshlight toy. "Then you get this." She sends him the evil eye. "It's the closest thing to pussy, you said, right?"

"Yes, it is." His expression is playful, but sheepish.

Brad grasps her harness and pulls her to the bed. "Time to switch out your sex toy babe."

She plucks the toy from her pussy. It makes a slight pop sound. "Do we have other rules?" Anna spreads out flat on their giant soft bed and enjoys a nice long stretch. "I propose that we can't touch each other ... or talk." She relaxes her whole body as she maintains eye contact with him.

"Okay. I'll buy into that. We can make sounds, but no words." He nods as he lays back. He stands back up. "Well, shit, I guess I need to get naked too."

His manly chuckle is such a turn-on.

"About time," Anna retorts with a snigger. "Show me that fat cock."

He presses his fingers to his lips to remind her.

She watches with hungry eyes as her man strips down and bares his stunning erection. She opens her mouth to speak, but he presses a finger to his mouth once more.

She gives him a look of recognition and nods back.

She sips her champagne, which Brad has so thoughtfully remembered to place on her bedside table, then lays back, prepared to lose. This toy makes her come undone so quickly. And because she will lose with this toy pressed to her clit, she's resigning herself to losing this round. She shakes her head and holds a defeated sigh inside her body. It doesn't matter, aroused or not, this toy usually makes her come so fast it makes her head spin. She's convinced any attempt at resistance is useless; she's a goner. Well, hell, she just about lost downstairs anyway already so this is no stretch by any means. And she's primed so that puts her further along the arousal scale than Brad. She swallows her impending defeat like a good girl.

He points at her toy and then at her pussy. A silent command that is unmistakable from the Dom look in his eyes.

She grins and squirts a dab of lube on her bean. She presses the button to the first setting.

He raises an eyebrow and points his index finger toward the ceiling on repeat.

She presses her lips firmly together as she clicks the intensity to the next level.

He does his hand motion again.

She chuckles silently and obeys by putting it on the highest constant mode. She's toast. This will make her come in a minute with how far she is on the arousal scale.

She gives him the look that says he needs to do likewise and select the highest mode on his toy.

The touchdown of the unit on her clit makes her cry out. It's like going from nothing to almost max stimulation with this one.

He presses the toy over his erection and groans out likewise.

His sounds of enjoyment always shove her closer to the edge. Even more so now. She struggles to not climax. The battle is tough. She grits her teeth and squirms to try to distract herself from the all-out war this toy is raging on her ability to hold back. She's going to fucking come. And in seconds. The pressure becomes too much, her clit swells to fill the little hole in the toy. Here it comes.

Brad grunts and groans, sounding as if slightly enduring pain.

Anna's excitement tugs as the panic of loss of control spreads across her body.

"Truce!" Brad shouts in a loud enough voice to wake the dead. "Take it off now," he demands.

With a huge sigh of relief, she yanks the toy off her clitoral head.

"Fuck," she mutters quietly, assuming their silence is now over.

"I was going to come."

She rolls towards him, refraining from admitting it was so with her as well. "So!" she drags a finger along his chest and meanders it through his chest hair. "That's the point. I'm calling that a cheating move, mister." She plays with his chest hair, tangling it around her finger then releasing it, then giving it a tug.

"Well, maybe it is. But we are moving on to the second part of this round. We will give it twenty minutes, then if neither of us comes, we will eat dinner. Deal?"

She nods emphatically. "Deal."

"Okay, so here's the plan. We are going to play hide and seek. The one who is hiding has to use their toy until they are found. If you come while being seeked, you lose."

"Wait, this won't work. We will hear the hum."

"Nope." Brad stands up and digs in his bedside table drawer. "We will both be wearing earplugs." He opens his hand and shows her the bright green foam pieces in his palm.

"Oh, Brad! You are seriously a sexual genius! How do you think of these things?"

He laughs heartily. "You. It's all you, babe. You are so open and never shun my ideas, so they just flow."

"Magic. Pure magic." She grins back and snatches the two little cones of foam from his hand. She slips them into her ears, but then removes them. "This will work."

He purses his lips and nods. "Let's flip a coin to see who hides first."

Brad digs in his big mug and locates a quarter. He holds it up and flips it around. "See, a legit quarter."

"I'll take heads."

"Cause I want your tail."

She rolls her eyes but bites her lower lip. "You had to."

He sucks in his lower lip. "Had to," he agrees. He makes a goofy expression. "And you'll take my head alright."

"Oh, the cheese is getting extra runny now!" She pretends to be annoyed.

"I thought you liked cheese."

"I do." The ruined cheese sauce plagues her mind. That really does annoy her that she wrecked such a tasty sauce. "I need to go back to the store tomorrow. Now I'm determined to make that sauce, and without a sex toy in my pussy."

"Whatever you want to do, babe."

He flips the quarter. It lands. Anna grimaces.

"Fuck," she mutters. "My luck sucks."

"You've come so many times today, baby, I think your luck is on fire."

True. He had her there.

"I see a flaw in this plan." Anna taps her forefinger to her temple.

"Let me finish explaining." His appreciation of her analysis apparent across his face.

Of course, he has thought of everything. She waits patiently for him to finish the setup.

"There needs to be a benefit for both ways. So, if you hide well, and I can't find you for five minutes, you get to fully dictate all the rules for round five, no matter what." He hands her the smartwatch she has charging on the dresser.

She slips the smartwatch on and secures it. She nods slowly as she lets this caveat sink fully in. "So, if I hide easy, I may last staving off coming and not climax, so that's the benefit because I will have potentially won the round. But, if I hide in a hard spot, I might come, but get to decide the next round of play's rules?"

"Yes, precisely. So, we each are forced to make a choice." His grin is full of satisfaction. "Okay. I will give you approximately two minutes to get in your hiding place. Then in your spot, you must start the toy and I will look for you."

She squeals with excitement as she hops off the bed. "This will be fun. I never would have thought of an adult hide and seek game like this. You are brilliant!"

He bobs his head up and down. "I've got this arena covered. New sex games and situations are my forte."

"Indeed, they are." She'd hit the motherload in Brad in so many ways it was as if they'd been created for each other. She knew that might be silly, but it didn't change the fact that it was true.

She slips out of the room like she's a prowler and carelessly tears down the stairs. She's not making it this easy for him to find her by staying upstairs. No way. Her decision waivers, or should she? She looks around frantically for a suitable spot to hide, but everything looks like a bad idea. Her heart is racing as she tries to keep track of time. It's impossible, even with the watch on her wrist. Plus, in her state of elatedness, hyperexcited is an understatement, as is the exhilaration of being about to be hunted surges through her body. Does she hide easy so the time she applies the toy to her clit is short? Or does she hide in a hard spot, risk climaxing so she can fully decide how the next round plays out?

In her panic, she darts into the garage. Nope. Too cold.

She hurries back into the house. Her mind is spinning. With all these hormones swirling around her body, she's going to come quick for sure. She opts for easy and huddles in a semi-easy hiding spot behind the dining room table. She gasps. This is way too easy. She slides into the small space behind the recliner in the sitting room at the front of the house. She will only be visible when he comes in through the kitchen walkway to the room.

She agonizes if she made the right choice as she presses the toy to her clit. She senses him walking around now and her heart races like she's about to be tackled. The thrill of the chase while being still, but while stimulating her clitoris is almost too much. She shifts back and forth on her feet in her hunched-over state.

Time stands still.

She begs for it to hurry. Her arousal is near peak level. She holds in her moans as she twists her body. The dance of not coming is so delicate, it's like only a pin prick holding her back. The pleasure comes in waves and relief comes when it wanes. She's really become a master of control over her own orgasms after all the orgasm play she and Brad have done. But there are times when she is powerless and becomes so gripped, so consumed by her impending release, that she completely crashes into her orgasm, vulnerable and helpless. Those are the times Brad gets the most satisfied and satiated because he cherishes her loss of control. He always says it's his topmost favorite expression that spreads across her face.

An odd sound causes Anna to turn her head. It's not like a sound she had expected to hear. It's not low like Brad's voice. It's something else.

As she fully pivots, her heart stops.

Her eyes flare open wide and she falls to the floor. In the exit from the kitchen stands her sister, and Brad appears in the other entrance to the room, naked, and holding his fleshlight in his left hand.

Anna scrambles to pull the earplugs from her ears and hide her uncovered mound. Not that she really cares if her sister sees her, but it's instinctual after being caught naked, with a sex toy in her hand. She glances down at the harness adorning her body. A bubble of laughter births in her gut.

Her sister's face is aghast, tormented, and fat with disgust, like Anna had just flashed her naked body to an entire church congregation. She takes a few steps backward, covers her mouth with her hand as the full horror of what she's seeing floods her face.

The text Anna ignored earlier sneaks itself into her awareness. She bets it was Madison texting her that she was stopping by. Well, shit. The ridiculousness of the situation causes Anna to burst into a loud cackle of hysterical laughter.

Brad laughs too.

This only infuriates Madison further. Her face goes red, angrier, and then she turns to run out of the house.

"Madison, wait," Anna calls after her sister. Anna rises to her feet to try to block her sister from leaving so she can explain, not that it will likely help the situation, however.

Madison shoots her another disapproving look, like she's some vile lowly dirty creature, which Anna has grown used to since her declaration of intent to divorce, and she skitters out the door faster than an admonished child flees.

Anna stands at the open door and calls to her sister again as the cold winter wind slaps her bareness in sharp stings. She waves wildly at her sister as she backs out down their driveway. Anna closes the door as her laughter churns into a deep guttural belly laugh, which Brad mirrors.

"Oh, my fucking gawd!" she exclaims when the laughter subsides.

Their gazes meet as they continue to enjoy the insanely funny scenario with peals of jubilance.

"That was epic," Anna says. "Did you see her face?" She erupts into laughter again.

Brad's hysteria finally settles so he can say, "That was the absolute best ever. She was so ... " He blasts into a fit of laughing again.

They both stumble towards the couch in the living room as they try to regain control. The fire is flickering in the fireplace and Anna is grateful for the warmth across her bare skin.

"I will never get over that look on her face. That gasp." She loses control again in a fit.

After they both come down off the comedy high. They embrace.

"Well, live and learn. That was the perfect storm." Anna grins deeper. "Honestly, I have a confession."

"Oh? Do tell." Brad's face transforms into an anticipatory swell. "I'm excited to hear this."

"I kind of, well, really for sure, absolutely loved that this just happened. It's like a smack in her face after all the shaming she did to me about the divorce and marrying you."

Brad's grin is full. "I can totally appreciate that."

"She shamed me so much, pushed me too far, so that I no longer care what she thinks. But I must say, I'm so happy to stick it to her like this. She saw us having fun. Being playful. Being sexual. Things she's told me she wants in her own marriage. So, I know this will grind on her."

"I understand your enjoyment of what just went down. And I'm very happy to hear you've released more of her hold over you." Brad was always way too generous with her sister. "Do you think you will ever be close with her again?"

"No. She's ruined too much. I no longer care, so she can't shame me. She can't even admit to some of what she said to me. I'm not playing that gas-lighting game of hers anymore. She's lost my respect and trust."

"Yep. She has. There's no doubt."

Anna sighs. "Well, this round got sabotaged as fuck. I was actually about to come when I noticed her. I mean, these earplugs work pretty good, but I heard a weird sound and it was her scream." Anna snickers. "I panicked at first, then I couldn't not laugh. She looked like a cartoon character. Her expressions changed so fast."

"Yeah, I didn't see her initially, but when I did, it was very funny."

"She's so judgmental, this was like a gift to have her walk in on, seriously." Anna can't stop the absolute glee from flooding her face. "I love that she got to see firsthand how playful and happy we are together. Maybe she will finally shut up about me giving up on my first marriage. But really, I don't give a fuck what she thinks, but I love sticking it to her with this. I couldn't have asked for a better revenge for how she treated me." Anna hugs Brad. "It's poetic justice. And I didn't even have to do it intentionally or slap her in the face with our happiness either. I mean, I'm not that cruel. Even though she rather deserves it."

Brad squeezes her. "And that you are wearing this harness is like the cherry on top."

"I know, right?" Anna exclaims with pure bliss loaded in her words. "She's such a prude. My outfit alone probably scared her."

"I love the unexpected turns and surprises this day of play has brought us. It's turning out even better than I had imagined it would. I'm having a total blast. You?"

"Oh, Brad. Yes. Yes, a million times, to the moon and back. I'm loving this day so much and I'm loving you more and more every second."

He puffs out his chest and points at the ceiling. "I declare this round done and a tie. I'm starving. Let's get dinner going before I eat the whole loaf of bread in one inhale."

She gives him a coquettish look. "I'd like to see that, actually."

He guffaws. "What? Me with a big loaf of bread sticking out of my kisser?"

"Like a cock?" Anna bites her lower lip.

"I love how you turn everything into an innuendo. You give me a run for my money and I'm really really really good at making everything about sex."

"And that, my love, is one of the reasons I'm so very crazy about you."

They make the remainder of their dinner while munching on bread and salad, sipping on wine as they wait for the chicken and vegetables to cook. Then they settle into the table Brad set up in the living room in front of the fire so they can eat naked, and warm.

The firelight flickers across their candlelit table.

"Perfect."

Brad's relaxed eyes reach his mouth as he blooms into a savoring smile. "Perfect, just like your nipples by the light of the fire."

Book 5
The Limo Sex Challenge
Chapter 1

B rad checks his phone. Countdown to limo arrival is thirteen minutes. Anna is still naked. He smirks, wishing she could just remain naked for the ride. He's sure the limo driver wouldn't mind, but damnit, she might need clothing.

"Babe, my surprise is almost here, but it means you must have clothes on. As much as it pains me to say this, it's true." He rubs his hands together as she reacts. "Time to get dressed."

She cackles with delight. "Well, this is a first. You're telling me to get dressed rather than undressed."

He grimaces as he glances down at his own naked bod, realizing he definitely needs to dress too. "I know. Who am I? Right?" It does feel foreign and just plain wrong to get her into clothes rather than out of them.

Anna dances around the living room, nude in the fire's flicker, her breasts bobbing seductively as she swivels her hips to the music. He wants to tackle her to the ground and fuck her right in front of the fire, but the limo will be here soon. No time. Plus, it isn't time for that quite yet.

"What shall I wear?" She winks at him and purses her lips for a kiss to the air. "Lingerie?" Her eyes are lit and her expression is playful. She's gorgeous.

She's got him now, though. He has to give her clues about what is about to happen. Or does he? Even if he's paying the limo driver so he can sit in the driveway for a few minutes, waiting as she gets dressed, who the fuck cares?

Brad raises his eyebrows as his eyes light up with his genius thought. "On second thought, stay naked." He knows how to play this without revealing the secret to her yet. Staying naked is the answer.

She frowns as a perplexed expression radiates out of her eyes. "Huh? What? Now I'm really confused." With her hands on her hips, he can't help but imagine his own hands there on her svelte curves, guiding her into a doggy fuck. His cock twitches. Fuck, he wants her doggy.

"Be a good girl and keep dancing for me." He settles on the couch as his cock stands upright once more. He's enjoying her dancing so much, why not savor her like this while they wait? Limo sex has always been a fantasy of his and he's more than tempted to just fuck her in the limo and call this a done day for their day of play. But that would go against the plan, and he is a man of following through on what he has planned. However, this irks him. Finally, he has a woman who will do such things as fuck in a limo and now he's got a limo coming and he can't fuck her in it? How did he end up screwing himself over like this?

She snickers as she plays with her breasts before spinning to point her ass at him, which she then shakes. She's so animated, it tickles his joy.

"Come get me, Daddy," she taunts in a sexy voice.

He groans. "You aren't making this easy for me," he mutters in an annoyed voice, while trying not to smile. It's impossible to not smile at his lovely wife. He wants to stroke his cock as he watches her seductive moves, but that will only make not coming harder so he refrains.

Four minutes to limo arrival. Hurry the fuck up limo driver because this is pure torture, not that the limo won't be. He shakes his head with a massive grin. Way to box yourself in, fucker. The edging he will endure will be worth it, though, when he finally penetrates her lush cavity and makes her scream, coming on his cock.

"I see that smile. You can't stay stoic with me." She charges him and plops herself on his lap, sandwiching his hard-on between both their bodies. "Why do I have a feeling I'm going to win this round?"

He groans heavily at the highly arousing addition of her flesh surrounding his cock, her tits in his face, and her lively jubilant eyes connecting with his. This whole situation is pushing his lust to bust out the ceiling. If the limo weren't coming ...

He stands up, which erupts her from his lap. He grabs her arms, so she doesn't fall.

"Whoa! A lap-sitting rejection?" Her bewildered look is super cute. "What's really going on here? You aren't acting normal." She accuses him even more with her eyes than with her words.

He ignores her and speeds to the front door. She follows him, right on his heels.

"Oh, where are we going?" she asks curiously. "I wanna play. Is this follow the leader?"

He stops in his tracks and swivels. His cock swings like a rod and smacks her.

"Oh, I want that," she says playfully as she reaches for his dick.

He laments his rushing to the door. He can't go to the front door now and watch for the limo, this would be too big of a clue. He retreats back into the living room, but he's sure as fuck not sitting down because he can't resist not touching her with her on his lap again.

"You are super turned on right now, I can see it in your eyes," she chides with pleasure. "And in your hard cock." She pokes at his back as they walk.

He bites back a smile.

He can't fool her.

He wipes his face clean to innocence before he turns around. He reaches for his phone on the end table next to the couch and hides it from Anna as he texts.

Brad: when you get here please park in the driveway and honk

Limo driver: I'm here. I'll honk.

Oh, he's early. Good. Let's get this show on the road. He lets his face show how pleased he is as he grabs Anna and plants a kiss on her lips.

She squirms in his grasp as a horn blares from outside.

"Oh! What was that?" Her eyes flare into saucers. "Is someone here? That sounds really close to the house."

She pries herself from his arms and dashes to the front door like an excited kid on Christmas morning. He follows.

Even though she's naked, she flings the front door open, and he loves her all the more for it. She's fearless.

She squeals and claps her hands. He'd do all this again just to see her react like this on repeat. All her juicy curves flop deliciously as she continues to bounce in excitement.

"A limo! Oh, my gawd! Brad! You are a genius!" She spins to face him and clobbers him with her naked body, clinging to him with her legs wrapped around his hips like a baby monkey. He grabs her and supports her full weight.

She plants kisses over his face as her hands scrunch his hair between her fingers. She leans back as he holds her securely with his arms firm against her back. He scans her flesh with a ginormous smile. This is his version of heaven. Her mauling him with kisses while naked and exuberantly happy, and plus, turned on.

"I love you! You keep surprising me today! You are the best husband on the planet!"

His heart glows brightly as her words warm not only his insides but, in fullness, his soul. They really are the most perfectly matched couple. He's so hugely blessed he often wonders what he did right to get the stars to align for him and Anna to meet in the first place. He's not that lucky usually. Thankful doesn't even begin to describe it, meeting her literally saved him from desolate and lonely misery.

"I'll never stop surprising you." Not with that look in her eyes beamed his way. He'd love to see that brilliance every day for the rest of his life, should he be so lucky. He fully intends on aiming for that.

He pats her right bare bottom butt cheek with one hand while still supporting her on the left with his other.

"Time to get some clothes on, babe." He regrets that he has to say such a thing to her again.

He sets her down and she scampers upstairs like a baby squirrel, squealing with elation the whole way.

He grins deeply. This is the best level of the game yet and they aren't even inside the limo.

They both dress quickly, her in the little black dress he had laid out for her earlier when she was finishing their dessert. She had planned to make an apple crisp when they were in the store earlier, but he couldn't have told her then that she didn't need to bake a dessert, that they'd be going out for it later. In the limo. No matter. They'll eat the apple crisp tomorrow. She is a terrific cook and baker, but tonight is about getting dessert in a limo. He'd hit the lottery with her and every damn day he learns this more and more. He never thinks his happiness can be topped with her, but she continues to prove him wrong daily.

"I can't wait to see what else you have planned."

Her giddiness is contagious. His anticipation thickens.

Her eyes shine as if on fire. He's always been fascinated by the magnitude of the zest in her eyes; it practically glows out of her like a brilliant star on a black sheet of sky does.

"Even if you have nothing else planned, I'm beyond excited about the limo ride. What a treat on a boring, normal, winter Saturday." She pauses her dance across the bedroom. "Well, this is certainly no ordinary Saturday, though." She cackles.

She's not wrong.

He nods slowly as he finishes pulling his trousers up. He fiddles with his tie, realizing it doesn't really matter, but why not make it nice?

"And to dress up for this too? How fun, Brad!" She's so lit up it makes him beam.

He relishes his idea of adorning nice clothes as she presses her breasts to his backside, before shooting her hands up the lapels of his suit. She gives his pecks a squeeze and thrusts her pelvis up against his ass.

He chuckles, recalling how he did that to her earlier, remembering how it turned her on so immensely. He yearns to do it again. It takes everything in him to not throw her on the bed and consume her. Clasping her hands beneath his forearms, she hums happily. He sways them back and forth as a unit.

"Let's go on a winter wonderland ride, babe." He grabs her hand, twirls her around, and then pulls her along. "Your body being my wonderland."

"Yes," she agrees. She scurries along towards the front door and he follows dutifully.

At the bottom of the stairs, he points to the door. "Stay here. Don't move. I'll be right back."

Her happy little sounds as she plants herself in front of the door bring him more joy than he feels he deserves. He scurries out of the house. Once in the garage, he opens the cupboard and grabs the packed picnic basket he hid inside yesterday. He flips up the lid and swipes his hand across the cold champagne bottles he nestled there ten minutes ago. He ensures Anna's thong is still around the chilled bottle on the bottom of the basket, as is the isolated little bag of ice he snuck in there not more than eight minutes ago to chill it. This ice would serve two purposes, keeping the bubbly cold, and sensation play. He can't wait.

"Perfect," he mutters happily as he closes the lid.

Anna is peering out the front door at the limo. Brad enjoys the view of her cute tight butt in the tight dress. He can't resist copping a feel of her firm bum.

"Mmmm, that feels nice," she murmurs seductively while meeting his gaze.

"Wait until you get into that limo, babe," he says with a bun squeeze. "I'll give you all the nice feels."

"Nice? Well, I sure am hoping for something way more sexy than nice!" she replies in mock anger.

"Oh, I won't be. You know me. This dress isn't staying on for long."

"What's in the basket?" she asks with a piqued look of interest on her face.

"Goodies for the ride. Let's go," he says as he holds the door open for her.

She shivers immediately as the cold floods the entryway. "Damn, I'd better make a run for it in this skimpy dress. This is going to suck." She shivers again and zooms out the door, her hair flying up as she rushes across the icy sidewalk.

Brad cringes, waiting for her to wipe out on the ice and break a bone, but she makes it safely inside the limo still upright. He locks the front door and takes his time walking. No need for a broken ankle or wrist from slipping and falling on the ice to ruin this amazing day.

He nods to the limo driver, who has opened the window.

"Ready to go?" asks the limo driver.

"Yup, you've got the plan I emailed you, right?"

He grins. "Yup, got it, maestro. Good to go."

"Awesome. Thanks." Brad nods. He had struggled with how to assess the driver for willingness over email to allow sex in his limo. In the end, he decided to just try it and beg for forgiveness if caught rather than ask for permission. They'd get further on that route anyway.

The limo driver salutes. He seems chill enough. He had told Brad he'd do the ride himself to make sure it went off without a hitch.

Chapter 2

Inside the limo, Anna has nestled herself into the back seat. She looks sexy and cute all at once. Her grin makes Brad so pleased with himself. This is a really good idea. He fondles her breasts before even sitting. He smiles deeper as her face flits into a wanton expression. Yup. A really, really good idea. Brad drinks it all in with lush appreciation and satisfaction. He's going to fuck her good soon and then bathe her in his luxurious aftercare, and take damn good care of his girl.

"It's nice and toasty in here." She leans into his fondling of her boobs. "And your touch helps too."

He drops his hands to arrange the picnic basket and she captures her boobies to maul herself in his place.

"Yes, it is. And I can't wait to do more of that." He raises an eyebrow as he settles in the seat next to her. "That's my job."

She releases her breasts. "Indeed, it is. I'm all yours."

He loves that she fully submits to his sexual leadership. He couldn't be her dominant in the bedroom if she didn't willingly and happily submit, without any coercion or guilt. This way it's rich and full, not partial, with walled-off sections. He's done with duty sex and a sexless life, thanks to her. He'd come to understand that dominating her wasn't about winning either. They were both winners and they won every day by giving each other their love, not by the getting of it. It's a jewel in the chaos of his life that she does submit and give him her love. He also gets it that he's a very lucky man. Well, previous chaos, that shit was now done. Life has rounded out to a pleasant daily experience with her. And he can't wait to enjoy his upcoming retirement with her at his side. His only question is when should he initiate that realm of his life.

"You look so gorgeous in that dress. Just beautiful. And sexy as fuck. I could eat you." He gives her a lecherous look. "And I think I'll do just that."

"Anytime," she says gleefully, like she's ready for that to happen any second now. Seemingly unaware of her actions, her thighs part. He likes that instinctive move very much.

The limo pulls out and turns onto the main road as Brad grasps the top bottle of champagne. "Might as well start enjoying this while it's still chilled."

"Hot chocolate might have been a better idea, but now that I'm in here, I am warm. Damn, it's getting worse out here." She shudders as she glances out the window.

"It is." Brad wishes he'd grabbed their coats in case of car trouble. "Good thing for car heaters in Minnesota."

She nods. "Why do we live here again?" she asks, cajoling.

"Kids and upcoming grandkids." Brad pops off the cork and the fizz puffs out the top in a little cloud.

"Yup, you nailed it. This kind of weather makes me want to turn into a snowbird, though."

"That could legit happen." He smiles at her. This is already in the wheelhouse of his plans someday. Images of Anna lounging in a bikini poolside and on the sand next to the ocean form in his brain. Then a fantasy of fucking her as the waves caress her ankles on repeat wakes up his cock even more. "I'm feeling the formation of a plan right now."

She caresses his cock. "And I'm feeling the formation of something else." She bites her lip as she fondles his swelling cock.

"You get me hot faster than anyone I've ever been with," he says, knowing full well he's told her this many times. But the sheer elation it brings to her face each time he says it is worth repeating to infinity. Making her really feel her sexiness makes her so hot, insatiable, and he enjoys making her feel amazing, so he compliments her all the time. Well, it's not compliments, it's the truth.

They embrace and fall easily into a French kiss, their tongues tangling as their hands roam each other's bodies. They make out for a few minutes as the limo lumbers along. The wind whips the sides of the vehicle, making it shift against its power.

"Sounds nasty out there," Anna murmurs in a soft voice.

Brad wonders if she's warm enough yet for icy panties. "Warm now?"

"Very." She shimmies her shoulders in his hug. "You always get me nice and warm."

He can't get enough of her, which is a blessing compared to what he used to feel, wanting to get away from his partner all the time. This is a much better way to live life.

"Same here." He kisses her neck as she melts in his arms, relaxing her body and falling flaccid to his nuzzling of her neck. "Might need to make a mark to commemorate this drive." He loves that this turns on her as much as it turns him on to do it. He grunts and sucks her neck, but not enough for a hickey, not yet anyway. "Soon," he whispers against her skin.

"I'm yours and I love it when you mark me." Her tone is full of savoring in its breathy essence, almost moan-like.

He'd never got off on doing such a thing before to a woman, but with Anna, he is always free to be himself and to bring up new things without fear she will fly off the handle or get pissy. They both knew what they wanted after having years of what they didn't. It's pure bliss for him, and she confirms the same to him all the time. He gets to be more of himself with her and he constantly surprises himself even. Things he didn't realize are turn-ons for him have the opportunity to thrive with Anna, and he sees the same phenomenon in her. The openness of their marriage allows such great freedoms as he hasn't even fathomed before.

"You are my perfect match, babe." It's not enough to say it once.

"Same," she says as she dips her head back, falling slack, losing her composure from his mouth tasting her flesh.

He sits up and fills their champagne flutes. "Guess I got distracted." He hands her a full glass and they clink their glasses together. "To wintery days that are perfect for a day of sex challenges."

"To a day of play," she says before taking a sip. "Mmm, yummy." She takes another drink before fixing her eyes on him. "What else is in that basket?"

He loves that he's got her curious. "You shall soon see." He almost empties his glass. "But first, a little nip nibble while the champagne is still on my tongue."

She slips her dress down quickly to offer her nipple to him.

"Fuck, I love your nipples." He devours her taut peak and caresses it with his tongue before sucking her deep to the back of his throat.

Her pleasure sounds deepen the harder he sucks. He could suckle her all day if she'd let him. His cock stiffens more as he mouths her tit. The champagne flavor lingers as he savors the taste of her body, the aroma of her pussy, the arousing press of her body to his.

He pops off her tit. "Pour a little champagne on your boob as I suck you. I'll slurp it in." He grins, loving his idea.

She squeals as the drink hits her flesh. She squirms as he sucks harder to pull the cool beverage into his mouth.

He moans out his enjoyment of tasting her skin and the champagne at once.

"I'm going to be all sticky," she says in a breathy, alluring voice.

He chuckles lightly. She's not wrong. The wind flares against the walls in wild gusts. He prays the potential snowstorm in the forecast holds off until they get back home. Stuck in a snowstorm while fooling around in a limo wouldn't be nearly as much fun or enjoyable, but at home, bring on the storm. It makes intimate times even more cozy when safe inside the house with a raging snowstorm going on outside. If only the weather were as predictable as his desire for Anna, and hers for him.

He continues to have fun playing with her nipple in his mouth as he fondles her other breast and body, her hands deep in his locks pressing him to her. He relishes when she pulls his face in like this.

Her moaning sounds of enjoyment elevate his lust even higher as they get steamier in their entanglement. He'd love to dominate her right here in the limo and make her his by penetrating her pussy with his cock, but it's still playtime. That intense fun will be for later. His patience is wearing thin, though. He just really wants to fuck her. He mentally grits his teeth. He will make it to the end of the day before full intercourse happens or die of lust trying.

"Oh, Brad, that feels amazing, omigod." She writhes in the seat from his touch, from the contact and stimulation his adept mouth has over arousing her nipple. He'd learned well in his youth the absolute power of simultaneously stimulating a woman's nipples and clitoris at the same time. It's pure sex magic. He is ready to employ that pleasure for her imminently.

He drags his tongue over to her other nipple and properly tastes it. The soft music playing is a seductive tune he partially recognizes with a saxophone solo. It's the perfect mood for plumping up the sensuality.

With Anna's breasts now bare and her dress pushed down to her waist, baring her pussy for the sensation play will be swift and easy. He comes off her nipple with a mouth-smacking sound.

She smiles and giggles. "Mmmm you know exactly how to arouse me."

"Yes, I do. And I'll never tire of raging you to the peak." He licks her underboob where her skin is still glistening. Then he fills the champagne up to the brim and hands her the glass.

They sip as Brad relaxes in the seat, his hand on her thigh. They both lean their heads back and make eye contact. Taking a slight breather to slow things down is what he and his cock both need.

"This is a very luxurious level of our game today. You've outdone yourself, Brad."

"I would do this every day if I could. You are so sexy, my love. Do you know how sexy you are? I'm the luckiest man alive."

Her expression shows she's amused, but loves his gushing. "I'm the lucky one."

He rubs her thigh as they continue to stare into each other's eyes.

"My beautiful wife. And I get to say that out loud every day now." He's proud of the intimacy they've built together. It's not just sex, no checkbox fucking here, it's on a whole new level for the both of them. Talking about their sex together has become one of his favorite things to do. "You know, and I've said this before, but I'm going to say it again. You make it so easy to be me. I love watching your face when you cum for me. Seeing that vulnerability in you as you are fully submitting to the pleasure I'm giving you, it's a Dom's dream. Seeing you lose control because of my control is one of the best feelings in the world for me. Topmost really."

She nods as her smile beams and her eyes light up in agreement.

He knew too well that the word control can be a bad thing, but when it's right, it's a thing of pure beauty and rightness. But it had to be the kind of control that allowed her to be her true self, and him, too.

Her eyes fall half closed as he plays with her pussy mound through her dress, pressing his fingers into her padded flesh there. "It's amazing for me to be able to let go. To accept your guidance and direction. It's intoxicating and I crave it. As I said, I'm the lucky one." Her eyes fill with a happy knowing that she enjoys the same phenomenon in their marriage.

He pinches her nipple at the same time he presses above her clit. She gyrates her body, dancing in her seat to the nip-clit pleasuring he's offering. After a few minutes of the dual touch, he reaches for the picnic basket and pulls out the next bottle of champagne, which has her panties wrapped around it. "For this next bottle, we are starting the sensation play. Which begins with you putting on these chilled panties."

Her mouth falls into a big o.

Brad loves her shocked expression, but there's no resistance in it at all.

She scoffs lightheartedly. "What? Are you insane? It's freezing outside! The last thing I want to do is put cold panties against my warmed pussy." She's so aghast and he loves that he's succeeding in surprising her.

"This will be fun. I have something planned for us to do with ice cubes too. It's warm in here. And I'll keep you warm. Don't you worry." He slips the panties off the champagne bottle and kneels in front of her.

She readies her feet by raising both off the floor of the limo.

He slips the cold fabric over her feet and slowly, seductively, glides them up her shins. She shivers and squirms the closer he gets to her pussy. She raises up her buttocks as he nestles the panties against her folds.

She gives a small cry of reaction once they are snugly on, and he grins. He presses the fabric between her lips, and she releases a tiny gasp.

"Oh, that is cold." She shudders.

He presses the lace with his tongue and licks at her panty-covered slit and clit.

"I'm glad I'm warm because now I've warmed them up. And your hot tongue is helping that a lot." She raises an eyebrow at him as she asks, "Don't tell me we are opening any windows for sensation play because I'm out if that's the plan."

He chuckles. He knows she hates the winter weather. "Nope, that's not how we are rolling."

The limo continues roaming the countryside as the wind whips it, trying to make it veer off the road at times. He knows he'd better get a move on with his plan before they have to turn back due to nasty weather.

She gets on her knees and crawls between his legs, a look of pure seduction on her face. "I've always wanted to do this." With her tits still bare, she unzips his pants and takes his cock out. "Suck cock with a man in a suit and my tits bare, with only his dick out, and in a limo."

He sighs happily as he leans back, enjoying the thought of her taking the reins for a few minutes to give him head in the limo. "Well, I'm more than happy to accommodate your fantasy. And why didn't you tell me this one before? I'm so loving it."

She leans forward slightly, making her tits hang. She shakes her body, making them swing. "I have lots of fantasies, but I can't recall them all every second, silly," she says in a sassy way.

"Well, I'm really happy with this one, and I'm looking forward to finding out about all of them lurking in that sexy brain of yours." Truth be told, it had always been his fantasy to get head and have sex in a limo, and to have her fantasy match, he is more thrilled to be getting this right now.

She maintains eye contact as she takes his cock head into her mouth. With her hands wrapped around his hardened dick, she rides him with both slowly, then speeds up. With her head bobbing in his lap and the sensations she's inducing in him, he almost comes. In mid-grunt, he forcefully pulls her off his cock and she falls back with an aghast look on her face.

Her expression is of utter surprise to have been flung so harshly off him.

"Whew, fuck. Sorry babe, I almost came. Had to stop you. Whew! Holy shit." He's panting and he catches his breath before saying, "That was hot. Holy fuck me."

She looks pleased with herself, bites her lip, and crawls back towards him. "That's where I was supposed to have won this round, you know."

With her tits hanging down like that, he just wants to rail her from behind in a doggy fuck and make her scream loud enough for the limo driver to hear her through the wall.

She dips her head coyly to the side. "How about a little titty fuck?"

"You know all my buttons." He's afraid that he will come for sure now. She's playing hardball and he's a goner.

She wraps her breasts and rides him with enjoyment consuming her face. "Just a mini ride," she says innocently.

But, true to her word, she stops and climbs onto his lap.

Once she's settled in, he says, "Now let's get those damn panties off you."

He hooks his fingers into the elastic and begins to slide them down her warm thighs.

"Now that I've warmed them up, it's time for them to come off?"

"Yup," he says with a deepening, explicit grin. "The next chilling stage is up."

Chapter 3

She kneels on his lap as he slides the panties off her, one of his favorite things to do other than bare her breasts. Well, then there is also the baring of her ass, but who needs to pick anyway? If the limo driver is looking at his camera, he's now getting a nice shot of her ass and pussy lips. He admits that he heartily likes that. The limo driver wants to be him.

She stands up and he drags the panties down to her ankles and off her feet, one at a time.

"Since I'm half naked, do we now half undress you?" She reaches for his tie and flips and tosses it about in the air.

He leans forward and removes his jacket and begins to unbutton his shirt. She pushes his hands aside and slowly undoes each button, her eyes securely connected to his.

"One by one," she says playfully as she continues to unbutton his shirt, kissing his newly exposed flesh as she descends. "Thanks for not wearing a t-shirt."

"All for you."

He slips his arms out of the shirt once she's undone all the buttons and shoves off his underwear and pants in one fell swoop. "Make your mouth cold with champagne and we'll get this going."

She sits on the floor of the limo and sips her drink heartily at his suggestion. He does the same. Then he pats the seat next to him. She gets comfy as he slides her dress up her legs to expose her bottom and pushes her to lay back on the seat. Once her dress is around her waist like a belt, he grabs the bag of ice.

"Warm enough? Or do you want the heat turned up?"

"Maybe one notch up, yeah." She hugs herself. "Ice play in a limo on a freezing cold day is like an oxymoron."

"Yep," he says with a chuckle. "I've succeeded in surprising you though."

"That's for sure, and I love it, Brad. I truly love this day."

Brad soaks in her comment. He admits, she makes him feel like a man. He examines the controls and sets them to her wishes. "Okay, this challenge is a sensation challenge." He unzips the bag and pulls out an ice cube. "First up, are your nipples."

She shivers before he even touches the ice cube down. "Well, shit, this will make me squirm."

"My thoughts exactly," he says with obvious enjoyment. "My goal always." He presses the square ice cube to her right nipple, and she cries out.

She tries to get away but being between the seat and Brad, there's nowhere for her to go. She gasps as he rides her wrinkled and dimpled nipple flesh and bastes the peak of her sensitive nugget with the melting cube. She squeals and pushes his hand, but he remains steadfast keeping the ice in place. He quickly pops the cube in his mouth and takes her nipple inside to join it.

She continues to squeak and writhe beneath him as the melted ice runs out his mouth and down her breast. He wets and chills her other nipple with another ice cube to her alternating sounds of protest and pleasure.

"Time to get you naked."

She titters a laugh. "I am naked."

"No, you're not." He gives her a dominant glare as he smiles. "You need to be fully naked. I still see a dress on you."

She lifts up her butt as he removes her dress, then flings it to the far end of the limo.

The limo jerks slightly and they both almost lose their balance.

"Whoa," she says with apprehension. "The roads must be slick."

"Yeah, and the wind has been pushing us around. Do you feel unsafe? Want me to tell him to head back home?" He'd end this in a heartbeat if she is afraid.

She shakes her head. "No, let's keep going. I want to see where this goes."

The curiosity in her eyes satiates him. He adores her adventurousness and willingness to try his ideas. Scratch that. It's not just a willingness, but it's a drive of hers. She thrives on his ideas and really immerses herself in them, which is a trait he fully cherishes. He shudders, thinking about what they'd be missing out on had they never met in person that day. He isn't sure he believes in fate, but he believes something had brought them together. Maybe it was God, maybe it was their souls tasting each other once in the presence of each other, but the draw of them had been something from the first time they were in each other's presence. It had been unmistakable, a sort of awakening of an awareness that he hadn't known he was missing, but fully took in immediately. There'd been this clicking of them upon first meeting, and it had only grown stronger and thicker with time.

"Okay, let's get to it then." He plucks an ice cube from the bag and presses it to her mouth.

She dances in place as she makes little mewling sounds. He pokes the corner of the ice cube between her lips and slowly presses it inside. Keeping eye contact with her, he does the same thing to himself. As he rotates his body, he knows she'll get what is next.

"Oh, I see," she says with excitement.

Settled into the sixty-nine position, she takes his cock in her hands and guides him inside her ice-chilled mouth.

He gasps as the ice cube rubs his flesh. Whew! It is a shocker. But the combination of her hot wet mouth and the ice cube is erotic. "Oh, damn," he exudes.

Before consuming her pussy with his mouth, he rides the cube along her slit.

She falls immediately off his cock and gasps out as the cold invades the warmth of her flesh. "Oh, fuck that's cold!"

He continues to ride her slit, slightly pressing it into her lower lips as she wiggles beneath him. As he rides her clit relentlessly with the ice, she cries out louder.

"Oh, my ... fuck!" she sputters out. "Oh, it's too much!"

He's not stopping now. With no safe word spoken by her, he pokes the cube into her hole as she thrashes beneath him but doesn't try to buck him off.

"Good girl," he says in his firm dominant voice. He snatches another ice cube and pops it into his mouth before handing her another one.

He hears the cubes rattle against her teeth.

They begin to suck each other's genitals with the ice cubes in their mouths. Their sounds are highly entertaining and arousing at once as they each groan and shriek out. Brad loves that neither of them are holding back and are being as loud as they want. If the driver hears them, he doesn't care; in fact, he knows it will turn Anna on if he does, which in turn, turns Brad on even more. They continue to simultaneously orally pleasure each other for several minutes as the wind whips the external shell of the vehicle. It's sounding even more voraciously nasty out there.

Her body lurches beneath his and he instinctively sucks her harder. Her movements tell him she's likely coming. She falls off sucking his dick with her sounds escalating to the point where he knows she definitely is climaxing.

Her body twitches beneath him as her sighs of arousal descent begin shortly after.

He's won this round, and that is a fantastic triumph. He's so very pleased with himself. He lives to make her come.

The limo jerks, taking a hard right, and the brakes squeal. They don't come to a stop but launch into a tailspin. The impact of the limo slamming into something throws them both on the floor of the limo in a heap.

Anna screams, "Oh my God, we hit something big."

Brad scans her quickly, assessing for damage. "Yes, damn. Shit. Are you okay?" He's trying to shake the accident off without sounding too alarmed. He wants to remain cool, calm, and collected for her to not scare her.

She nods with fearful eyes. "I hope the driver is okay."

"Me too." Brad scrambles to sit up. "Did you get hurt, babe?"

"No, I'm okay. I think we were going slow enough or that could have been much worse." She looks up at him in worried anticipation. "Are you okay?"

Brad nods as he sees cherry red lights stream through the back window of the limo.

"Well, shit, that was fast. A police car already?" He scrambles to reach for Anna's dress. He tosses it to her. "Better dress fast. He's upon us."

She dresses in a flash before he even gets his underwear on. All she had to do was slip her dress over her head though.

"Police must have been near and just saw this happen." She smooths her dress and her hair. Her expression is harried, likely because she just came in addition to the crash. "I'm shaking."

"From the orgasm or the accident?" he asks full of concern.

"Yes," she says good-naturedly. Her face and shoulders relax.

He's super thankful she's not freaked out.

"Not the end that I'd expected," he chuckles humbly.

"No, I was ready to make you come."

"And I won this round," he says proudly.

"No," she protests. "I didn't get my fair chance."

"I beg to differ, you almost made me come earlier."

She crosses her arms and huffs.

He gives her a triumphant grin. She can't deny it. She most definitely came. "I loved the ice during that. What did you think?"

"Yup, it sure made me squirm and scream."

"Exactly what I had hoped for." He fastens his pants and reaches for his shirt as there's a knock on the window.

"Are you guys okay?" It's the limo driver. He doesn't open the door.

"Yes," Brad calls out as he tries to frantically button his shirt as fast as he can.

With Anna calmly sitting on the seat put back together, he doesn't want to be the naked one.

"Do we need to get out? Is there any danger of engine fire? Any smoke?" Brad isn't taking any chances. He's not sure whether to laugh at this disaster or allow panic to reign, but he sure has both lurking around inside.

"Nope, I'm so sorry about this. Are you both sure you are okay?" His voice is full of worry. "There's an officer here."

Brad opens the door and a gush of cold wind rushes in.

Anna says, "Oh dang, that's brutal."

Brad pulls her into a quick hug to warm her up. "We are fine. Are you okay?"

The driver nods emphatically but with a sheepish expression. "I have to apologize before the cop gets out of his car. I was watching you guys too much." His face reddens and he makes a pained expression. "I'm really sorry. I ... "

Brad holds up his hand as Anna draws in a big breath. "No worries at all, my man."

He glances at Anna, who is beaming from ear to ear.

"She likes that," he says to her gasping.

"I can compensate you guys, give you a refund, just please don't sue me. This is my business." His eyes are full of worry that Brad wants to erase.

Brad snorts. "Sue you? Hell no. My wife loves that you were watching, honestly." He nods towards Anna, who aggressively bobs her head. "We have a bit of exhibitionism in both of us. So, no harm done. No one is hurt."

"Yes, yes, yes I do love it." Anna points to her panties which are near the door as evidence.

The limo driver relaxes immediately and smirks. "Oh. Seriously? Ok. Well, in that case, that was a nice move there. Might have to copy you at home with my wife." His eyes are amused as he raises both of his eyebrows. A wind gust moves through the area and his hair flies up in wild abandon. "After I get towed home that is. Once you guys get out, I'll try to see if it's drivable, but I already ordered you guys a lift."

Chapter 4

The police officer approaches and waves at them to stay inside. "I'll take care of this. Be right with you, folks."

Brad nods acknowledgment and pulls the door shut.

Both he and Anna burst into laughter.

"Oh, wow. He crashed because he was watching us?" She covers her mouth with her fingers, but her laughter spreads it wide open.

"Sure sounds like it. And I thought it was the icy roads and wind only. Guess not."

They both laugh together as the wind whips the car like a bodyless beast.

"Whatever will we do as we wait for our ride?" Anna asks in mock innocence.

"I can think of a few things, and I've got another bag full of ice."

The car door opens and the officer peers in at them. His expression is pleasant, his hair is gray, and his demeanor is in charge.

"Are you two okay in here?" He's an older man with a full beard and grizzled facial skin.

"We are perfect, officer," Brad pipes up. "No harm done. We are not injured."

"Okay, the limo looks okay, but I'm advising him to not even attempt to drive in this weather. The whole front is smashed in. We don't need to risk him having more car trouble or an engine fire." He strokes his beard as he scans the inside of the vehicle. "Looks like your romantic drive got cut short." His eyes soften as a chuckle percolates out of his mouth.

Brad grabs and shoves Anna's panties into his pocket. "Yeah, it sure did. But that's life. We got a good ride, though, so far," Brad says with his voice full of explicit suggestion.

Anna's face flushes but her eyes tell Brad she's loving the insinuation of the officer knowing.

"Well, good, nothing wrong with that." The officer taps his forehead. "No jackets? Y'all from Minnesota?"

Brad purses his lips, really regretting not grabbing their coats. "Yep, all our lives. We were in a rush, so nope, we forgot them. We were focused on other ... paraphernalia." Brad pats the picnic basket with the champagne bottle sticking out of it.

"Anniversary?" the cop asks amused even further.

"Nope, just regular winter fun," Brad says with a laugh.

"Smart man," he says with an understanding tone. "Very smart man indeed. Well, how about you two hop over to my car and wait for your ride to arrive? I don't feel comfortable having you wait in the limo, just in case. I could have driven you home, but the driver said he already called a ride for you."

"Understood. And yes, thank you." Brad collects the picnic basket and the other bottle, and Anna grabs the flutes.

She slips on her high heels and grimaces. "I'm not looking forward to going out there, especially in these shoes."

"It's a brutal one. Storm is coming on strong now." The officer steps back, allowing them space to leave.

As they exit the vehicle, the falling snowflakes begin to thicken.

Brad hooks his arm around Anna and they hurriedly make their way to the cop car as the wind whips them.

Anne shrieks as they get blasted by a strong gust. She almost loses her balance and Brad tightens his hold on her.

They scramble hurriedly into the warmed police car. Brad's mind drifts to sex in a cop car. It will never happen, but it's a fun fantasy.

"Imagine sex in here," he says in a seductive hush.

"I know, right? Would be hot. What would be fun is a quickie while he's talking to the limo driver." She smirks. "Cop car head?"

He guffaws, but she maintains her interested expression. He asks, bewildered that she'd actually consider this, "Wait. Are you serious?"

She nods, reaching for his groin. "With your head up, you will notice when he's coming."

He doesn't need much convincing for this. The taboo thought thrills Brad and his cock fills. "Should we dare do this? What if we end up in jail?" He truly is the luckiest man on the planet.

"We won't, because you will see him coming." She purses her lips. "Plus, he seems like the type who wouldn't care."

"True. But what if they have a camera in here?" he asks cautiously, looking around.

"Well, then they will get an eyeful." She maneuvers herself over his lap, hovering for a second before slipping her dress off her shoulders so her breasts hang down.

"Oh, fuck, I'm going to come in a cop car, aren't I?"

"Yes," she murmurs determinedly before consuming his dickhead inside her mouth.

He grabs her breasts and plays with her left nipple as her head hops up and down in his lap on his head. Her little sucking sounds drive him wild as he pinches her nip and tugs it. Her adventurous nature flares further as she hikes up her dress and molests her clit. Her groans and her humming brings him right to the edge of his climax. He begins to shudder, his climax taking him almost to spewing. He's going to lose control.

"Fuck! He's coming! He's coming! Stop!" Brad shouts as he shifts his hips down to get himself out of her mouth. He painfully slips his hard-on inside his pants as Anna yanks her dress up to cover her breasts.

They get covered up just in time two seconds before the officer opens the door.

Anna licks her lips and kisses the air towards Brad as the man settles into his driver's seat.

"I can see a car coming in the distance. It might be your ride." He glances in the back seat via the rearview mirror. "You two must be freezing. Especially you, ma'am."

"Yeah, it's very horrible out there, especially in a dress like this." The champagne still has a bit of a hold on Anna as she says, "At least he found my dress. It's better than being naked out there. That'd be deadly."

He utters a heckle. "No doubt. I believe that dress would be too, you women are a brave lot. Too bad your fun ended, though." The amused look in his eyes tells Brad he may have noticed Anna's head had not been upright as he walked over to the cop car. "The driver has a tow truck coming."

The limo driver has a hand up blocking the blustering snowfall from his face as he's walking toward the cop car.

The arriving vehicle's headlights come into a clearer view behind him.

"This storm is expected to get worse," the officer reports. "It'd be best to get off the road anyhow now and head home."

"Yup, finish up the day at home, as we had planned," Brad says with confidence.

"Good thing we have a dessert waiting back home," Anna says pleasantly.

"Yeah, I had plans to pick up dessert while we were out, but that's life. Best laid plans turn into better ones sometimes though." He makes eye contact with Anna as they continue to enjoy sharing in their secret. "Well, my beautiful, lovely wife, shall we head for home?"

"Yes, for sure," Anna says emphatically.

"Thank you for your help, officer," Brad says as he opens the car door.

The blustery wind billows into the car as they exit. They rush over to the SUV and hop in the backseat.

"Welcome, where to?" asks the driver jovially. He's a young guy in his twenties with a goatee and shaggy hair that sticks up on the front of his scalp. It bobs as he moves his head while talking. "Nasty out there."

"It is really nasty and getting worse. Thanks for coming out to get us." Brad tells him their address and he pulls out.

"Celebrating tonight?" the driver asks with interest.

"Yup, just celebrating a fun day with my amazing new wife. A day of nothing but play." Brad makes eye contact with Anna, whose eyes are full of mischief. What's she got going in that brain of hers now?

"Been a driver long?" asks Anna, making small talk.

"Yup, about a year now. I love the flexibility with school."

"College?" Brad asks.

"Yeah, I'm at the U of M. Junior year now."

"Nice." Brad figures he's about his son's age. "Great college job to have."

"I bet you've got some wild stories from driving." Anna gives a silent laugh as her hand flies over her mouth. "Some crazy stuff."

"Oh, yeah. You have no idea. I've had everything from puking people to people having sex to oral." He snickers. "I've even had propositions for sex. It's crazy what people will do. They seem to view my car as a place of freedom."

Anna spouts, "Wow! What did you do when the people were having sex?"

He chuckles. "I just let them. I mean, why the fuck not? It wasn't hurting anyone, I wasn't offended. I was more worried about the mess they'd make, but they were careful to not spill. Was actually pretty hot, if I'm being honest."

"Oh, I bet," Anna exclaims. "We were getting pretty close to that in the limo, honestly."

Brad loves her sharing their sexual escapades with a stranger, so he smiles at her as she spills their story.

"Yeah, he surprised me. Champagne. Chilled. And chilled panties. We were pretty hot and heavy before we crashed too."

"Oh, hell yeah. Limo sex is the best." He runs a hand through his hair. "It'd be something I'd do."

Brad watches his wife's face further. He savors her relaxed aroused expression. "That indeed we were. But we will head home and finish up this champagne in the living room in front of the fire."

"Hey, pick up where you left off if you want. Don't let me stop your fun. Don't mind me. Do you as you please." The driver sticks his index finger in the air. "Just don't make a mess please."

Anna and Brad exchange glances, considering. Brad rides his hand up Anna's thigh. Maybe just a bit of fingering as they make small talk wouldn't harm anything. If she's receptive, that is.

Anna smiles as he slides his fingers up her thigh. She situates herself, spreading her thighs for him, while still sitting upright. She grips his hand in excitement as he tickles his fingertips along the part of her lower lips.

He dips his finger gently into the divide to find she's extremely wet. He taps his fingers into her pussy puddle and brings them to his lips for a quick taste. He does it again and gives her a taste of herself while talking to the driver about his career path. He presses his fingers into Anna's wetness again then plays his fingers against her clit.

Her head falls to the side and her eyelids partially close. She presses her fingers into Brad's flesh as her arousal climbs. She squeezes his hand between her thighs as her lips part slightly open as if she might sigh.

"You an ice fisherman?" asks Brad, keeping up the small talk to cover up his playing with her pussy. He knows she likely won't be able to talk.

"Yup, just rented a fish house on Mille Lacs with some buddies last weekend. Was awesome."

The driver turns the car which makes Anna lean too far to the side, she's clearly so flaccid and loose. She recovers stiffening her body back up, her eyes fluttering open in surprise for a split second.

"Yeah, I've done that too. It's a great time. Whether you get fish or not! It's fun playing cards, cribbage, eating, and drinking. But it's always a challenge to sleep in those things." Brad flicks her bean with his forefinger.

"It is. And my friend snores so I need to have enough beer to just pass me out cold so I sleep through it."

"Yup, same. I have that kind of buddy too," Brad agrees as he presses his index and middle finger inside Anna's drenched pussy.

A small sigh escapes her lips, but since the driver is talking, he doesn't seem to notice. Brad starts to pump his fingers into her faster, making sure to hit her clit too. He knows she probably won't come again, but it's sure fun to edge her like this in this situation.

The Dom in him rages as he brings Anna closer to the edge of orgasm. This will serve to make her orgasm even harder later. Part of him wants her to climax now in the car and have to try to stifle her sounds, but the other part wants her to lose control and finish her orgasm at home, where she will be completely unhindered. He loves watching her come undone. It's like a drug to him. He can't ever get enough. They'd developed a safe word, but Anna didn't like to use it. Instead, she'd shared with him that she loved him pushing her boundaries, guiding her past what she thinks she can handle. The peaks she's reached have blown his mind, he can't even begin to imagine what amazing awe-inspiring experiences it's sent her body and brain through. And he's been the man to lead her there. That's a gift. He'd never stop leading her into new sexual ground. It's what makes his life so exciting and full these days with Anna by his side every day.

Brad can't get their limo ride off his mind. "Yeah, we were just having a fun day together. Like an extended day-long date," Brad explains. "Just put the ring on her finger last month." Brad pumps his fingers inside Anna faster yet and she makes a little squeak as she clutches his hand, digging her fingernails in.

He grins at getting her to this point and happily endures the stabbing pressure of her nails.

"Oh, you two are newlyweds?" the driver asks Brad.

"Yeah, second marriage for both of us." He keeps his eyes on Anna. He can tell she is close to losing control as her head lolls to the side and she presses his hand harder into her womanhood.

"Nice," he says nodding. "Kids?"

"Yep, we both do. Pretty close to your age, actually."

The driver turns into their neighborhood.

Brad reluctantly pulls his fingers from Anna and sucks on them before stating, "Brown house with the truck in the driveway, up here on the right."

Anna's panting begins to slow, but her eyes still show how turned on she is. Another few minutes and he'd have had her coming right there in the car. Which would have made him the double winner of this round, he has zero doubts about that.

The car comes to a stop in the driveway and Brad and Anna prepare to exit.

"Thanks again and enjoy that tip!" Brad salutes the young dude and he and Anna exit the car.

"Wow! Thank you! Have a fantastic evening!"

Anna stumbles at first, but the cold jars her awake to her senses and she darts towards the front door. Brad isn't far behind her. He fumbles for his keys as she shivers next to him holding her arms wrapped around her slim torso.

"Holy fuck this is cold," she says, her teeth chattering.

Brad swings the door open. "Go in, my beautiful sexy bride. That was an amazing and sexy trio of escapades in vehicles."

She enters, but then whips around and pulls him into a deep open-mouthed kiss, her right leg wrapping around him.

Chapter 5

"I want you now," she murmurs impatiently.

He sets down the picnic basket and prepares for her to hop up to claim his body with her legs. He holds her thighs firmly as he shuts the front door behind him. He carries her to the living room where their fire is still raging. He places her in front of the fire and lowers himself to rest between her legs. They continue to kiss hungrily, finally satiating their desire to do so that had raged the last half hour when they couldn't.

"You are my dream," she mutters as she allows her head to fall back.

He kisses her neck and thrusts his erection against her. He's already looking forward to his favorite part after he fucks her into a multitude of mind-blowing orgasms; the aftercare. It's honestly one of his favorite parts to take care of her after he's fucked her hard, when he knows she's fully sexually satisfied. He loves to push her buttons, rage her to new heights, make her body lose control as much as her mind. Then, when she's spent and cum-drunk on so many orgasms, he loves to swoop in and cradle her. Make her feel cherished, loved, cared for. Claim her as his to pleasure, use, enjoy, guide, lead, play with, and take her places no man has ever even dared, or could. She adores him playing with her body and her sensuality as much as he loves her doing it back to him. It's their relationship, their intimacy, and their full mutual trust that makes all this possible. He's never loved anyone as deeply as he loves Anna. And he knows it's only something that will happen with her, it's not possible with anyone else. They are a perfectly matched couple, which is something he gets now that they get to live the full and beautiful truth of all that.

"Please, Daddy, fuck me. I need your cock inside me." Her voice is sweetly whiny and pleading, a tone of voice that always gets him so hot he wants to jam his cock inside her and rage fuck her, as he does now.

"Soon, baby, soon." He has lasted this long in the marathon of sex play for the day, he can't lose sight of his plan now. But, damn, is he on the verge of giving in and doing exactly what she wants, because he wants it so badly too.

He almost caves his resolve, but he gathers up all his strength to resist her. "I promise, it will be soon, baby."

"I want it now," she insists in a pouty, wanton voice.

"I know, I do too. But be my good girl and wait. I'm not going to fuck you yet," he says in the tone that he uses when he's feeling most dominant.

She falls limp with an exasperated sigh. "I want your cock in me." She wraps herself around him and he almost caves.

He loves her pouty bratty impatience, but he pries himself from her warm eager body, which is no easy feat, and stands up. His cock is so hard it hurts. He's ready to come so he needs a break, or he will lose this round too.

"You are ready to come, aren't you? I almost did on the ride home," she admits.

"I know, and I almost got you there. A few more minutes and you'd have lost it right in his car." Brad snickers. "I contemplated having him drive me to a store so I could make it happen. Do you think you could have come like that?"

She nods slowly as she raises up on one elbow, her dress enticingly skewed, almost showing the pinkness of her right areola. "I do think I could have. I was really close. The champagne helped me loosen up," she says with humility. "You know how to get me there. I love how you know my body so well."

"You are my obsession, that's why I know."

"I do know, and I love it."

"But I can't blow it at this stage. So, let's slow it down a bit. I'll get us champagne, we can finish up the bottle to get you nice and juiced up to come as I fuck you into oblivion like a rag doll."

"Yes, please, and oh I'm so very, very ready for that." She yanks her dress to fully expose her breasts. "And I'm playing hardball now." She swivels her body and tugs up her dress to reveal her pussy mound, then she spreads her legs. "Daddy want?"

"Oh!" he exclaims. "Fuck, fuck, fuck. You know exactly how to drive me wild." He closes his eyes and turns. "But I'm not wavering. Champagne, conversation, and then dessert, and then I'll fuck you to within an inch of your life." He sneaks a peek back at her and then can't tear his eyes off of her. This is tough. Really tough.

Anna hums as she lies flat on the ground. "No one came this round. We are a tie again."

"Don't deny it. You came in the limo right before we crashed."

She gives him a haughty expression which turns into a happy look as she knows she can't pretend it didn't happen. "I know, I did, yes."

"And get ready. Next round I will make you come so many times. You will be the big loser who wins the biggest because I'm going to fuck you into double digits of orgasms and blow your mind, fuck you to the point of sleep."

"And I believe you, and I can't wait." She gives him fuck me eyes and plays with her pussy with one hand while molesting her left nipple with the other. "I could come right now with very little stimulation you know," she says enticingly, still not giving up.

For a split second, he considers running for a sex toy and making her scream his name, but instead, he composes himself and makes his way to the picnic basket he left by the front door. He takes it to the kitchen and pours them each a glass, taking note of the dessert on the counter, he cuts them each a piece.

He sets it all on a tray and carries it back to the living room, where Anna has planted herself naked on the couch.

He shakes his head. "I'm going to be powerless here really quick, aren't I?" His naked horny turned-on wife sitting on the couch is something he can't resist for long.

She points to her pussy between her open thighs. "She wants your cock now," Anna demands.

He releases a deep sigh. "Not yet, be Daddy's good girl and enjoy this dessert and champagne with me first," he says in his stern voice that melts her.

"Yes, Daddy," she says obediently, but her eyes still say, 'fuck me now'.

"I love you," he says as he hands her a champagne flute.

"And I love you, Daddy," she says in that voice that rages his lust to the max.

"You are mine, and the best thing that has ever happened to me."

"Same." She takes a sip after clinking his glass. "Is it time to fuck me yet?" She laughs. "I'm a bit impatient after all this build-up to be your fuck toy."

He scans her sexy naked body and runs his hand down his covered erection. "Oh, you will be, don't worry, and we will both sleep like drained sex fiends."

"I can't wait."

Stay tuned for the final installment of the Day of Play Sex Challenges with Anna and Brad where satiation means the culmination of their sexy day of fun ends with the most explosive orgasms, and the most loving aftercare takes them to even greater heights than they ever thought possible. It will be delicious, delectable, and oh-so-very satisfying. Come celebrate their love and enjoy their jubilant fuck that will end their day in the best way possible as this gorgeously explicit and fun erotic rom-com tale comes to an end.

Book 6
Taste of Victory
Chapter 1
Anna

Anna frolics around the living room, the light from the fireplace glimmering in the shimmery threads of her dress. She is as alive as she has ever been. A bit drunk on champagne, dessert, and orgasm hormones, she smiles at Brad, who is resting, smiling at her from where he's lounging on the couch. She loves his indulgence. His savoring of all her many expressions of sensuality, like twirling about like this on a whim, which she never felt comfortable even showing her ex. He had never appreciated her like Brad, not even remotely close. They were oil and water. Brad being the oil, her ex being the thin water that fell quickly through everything. The staying power just hadn't been there. And, worse, there was no savoring with her ex, although he certainly left his stain. But with Brad, she is free and open, and he loves her all the more for it.

She smiles. "I love you, Brad." Focusing on the now, the bliss of her life, she bends over slightly to create more cleavage and shoves her breasts up and down in an alternating pattern.

"Ah, now that's what I'm talking about. You are speaking boob man language now." His expression is delightfully salacious.

What Anna loves is that he may be a boob man, but he also loves other parts of her body, and he frequently tells her so. It is a wooing she always succumbs to, happily and lustily.

"When does the dress come off?" he asks with hope.

"Soon," she retorts as she whirls about the room, glazing her skin with the warmth of the fire. The chill running from car to car earlier still clings to her body with ghosts of shivers plaguing her. Part of her wants to just wrap up in

133

a blanket, yet Brad is talking about getting her naked. "And my dress has been off," she retorts like a smart aleck.

"I can help with that, you know," he snickers.

"I'm a bit chilled from all that running around in the wind. That was brutal without a jacket. Hell, I think that kind of weather is brutal, even when bundled up."

"Yeah, that's for sure. But that thin dress can't offer much warmth anyway. Might as well be naked," he says suggestively as he taps his temple. "Hmmm. That gives me an idea. Something we haven't done in a while." He stands up and rubs his hands together. "Just what the Dom in me has on tap. This will be perfect."

"Oh? Do tell?" Anna pleads coquettishly. A flare of excitement bursts inside her.

"Not yet. I want to get a few things ready." He rubs her arm as he gazes into her eyes. His demeanor tells Anna he wants to slow things way down and savor this golden evening time with her as much as possible. She loves being with a savorer. "You relax a bit. Maybe a mug of tea? Cider? Hot toddy? I'm bartender," he offers.

Warmth from his caretaking wraps her up and she feels herself beaming at him. "Yes." She presses her body to him and he envelopes her in a full body hug. "How about a hot toddy? More on the hot, weak on the toddy? I'm a bit schnockered still from the champagne."

He nods knowingly. "Ah, yes. Let's keep you in the feeling good state, but not drunk. I want you fully aware and awake for this round, not too sleepy. Not yet anyway." He gives her face a soft swipe, ending with a slow fingering caress of her lips. "I want you to fully enjoy every second of this round. So, one light toddy coming up, babe." He pauses. "A little cheese and crackers, perhaps?"

She shakes her head, but in hindsight, thinking about it soaking up the alcohol, she says, "Maybe one."

He releases her and makes his way toward the kitchen. She watches him in a reverie of all her hopes realized. "I'm one lucky girl," she calls toward the kitchen. She nestles into the couch and fits a soft fleece blanket around her thighs, making sure her toes fit under the blanket too. "I might fall asleep like this, especially with a warm drink."

"A snooze isn't a bad idea, babe. You will awake refreshed and ready for our finale. And it will give me time to prep."

Prep. She loves the sound of that. This round already sounds luxurious. Being married to a generous pamperer continues to blow her mind. She's used to being the one always doing, not the one receiving, that is until she met him. "Brad, you are so good to me. I sometimes think I'm in a coma and dreaming this life."

She's not sure he heard that, but no matter. His humming in the kitchen cradles her heart. He takes such good care of her, and in ways she hadn't even fathomed before living with him. In no less than a second, her eyelids feel heavy.

Chapter 2
Brad

Ah, she's asleep. Perfect.

Brad sets down the mug on the coffee table next to Anna and places a small plate over the top to keep the heat in. He takes the time to let the dog out for potty and settles her into the spare room with water and doggie snacks so they can have full privacy together without a dog nose sniffing where she shouldn't. He silently chuckles, recalling how much they had laughed so hard the time during sex when she had sniffed his butt during doggy. He loved how they could laugh during sex but then quickly get back to the fucking seamlessly. Damn, he loves fucking her. More than anything else in this world, he loves to make her come.

He watches his wife sleep on the couch, admiring her beauty and the innocence of her expression while asleep. After snapping a picture of her for his own personal collection on his phone, he swiftly makes his way upstairs. This will be so ideal. He can't wait to finish off this amazing day of play. One of his best ideas yet to devote an entire day to edging and sex play, and he isn't even done with his plans for the day.

His plan is simple. Over-the-top pampering followed by great dominant aggressive sex, where they will both come hard, her multiple times, and then tender aftercare to the point of sleep. It's genius. Plus, he knows Anna will eat it up and fully appreciate it. His desire to do it is so full he's practically bursting at the seams to get it in motion. One of his favorites is when she just conks out after sex. The mark of a truly good lover and Dom is when she's so satiated and spent that she just falls asleep. At least in his book, that is.

He readies the bath by locating his favorite bath bomb, Tropical Island, lighting a few candles on the edge of the tub, and getting the diffuser going with the concoction of essential oils he'd found online that promised to be an aphrodisiac. He'd never imagined he'd be a guy to mix up such a frivolous mixture, but the effect he's seen overcome her when she was immersed in the

136

aroma is worth it every time. This is a new one, and he can't wait to see her dreamy look.

He gathers her favorite soap and fluffy towels, a nice soft washcloth, and he starts the water. He blasts it on the hottest heat so it can cool while he begins the seduction downstairs. Seducing his wife on the regular had proven itself to be the most valuable approach. She became his sex doll to mold and pleasure, she relaxes so much, it's as if she's fluid. Then he arouses her to a peak of sexual tension, then the release. The release on repeat. A formula he rarely deviated from because with it she came so hard, as did he. But she did love novelty, as he enjoyed providing it. Today's events are proof of that.

He mentally makes notes of the day, reminiscing with a grin. What a day it had been! All the crazy mishaps, the fun surprises, and the satiation. And damn, is he ready to feel her pussy clamp down on his cock, deliciously milking him of all this edging. All the buildup will be worth it and will most likely appease his raging inner Dom as well. Having a woman who desires to fuck him is itself a new treat, let alone one who actually asks for it. He was used to silence and refusals to discuss sex and desires.

He puts away a load of laundry before going back downstairs, just to give her a little bit more of a snooze. He contemplates snoozing too and setting his alarm, but he's way too worked up and excited for his plan. He couldn't sleep. But his sleep will be heavy tonight after he comes, no doubt. He chooses music for later when she's in the bath, then heads downstairs to rouse his lovely wife from her slumber, with plans to make her climax so many times that she lays like limp lettuce. Fuck her to sleep. He chuckles at the idea of her body all floppy with sex hormones. It's a sound goal.

He runs his hands over her legs, then her torso and arms, collecting her hair in his palm and rolling it about. Lastly, he caresses her cheek.

She smiles and slowly squirms. A little moan escapes her lips as her eyes flutter open. "Mmmm. I fell asleep? I guess I needed that."

"Yes, you did." He continues to caress her arms, doing little circles with his thumb over the insides of her wrists.

Her smile deepens as he gently rubs her wrists. One of her erotic zones he'd found by accident one day when they'd been walking along the beach on a Florida trip. He'd been touching her in all the usual spots all day long, but on the sand, with their feet in the water, he had done this move and she'd melted further. Now he used the move often.

"You're amazing," she says with eyes full of love. "You let me sleep. You are a mirage. Right? I'm either dead or in a coma, and I'm dreaming you up."

"I could say the same thing of you." He settles in on the couch and pulls her onto his lap. "This is where you belong now."

"Mmm. I like this idea." She nestles into his body and glances up at him. "Is this phase one of this round's plan?"

"We both already did phase one. This is phase two." He reaches for the hot toddy, slightly spilling her off his lap. "We can't forget to share this."

He gives her the mug, which is still warm, but no longer steaming.

She takes a sip and moans out her pleasure. "Mmm. That's so warm and good."

She lifts it up to him.

He takes a slow sip, the warmth flooding his insides. "Damn, that is good. I didn't realize I was still chilled too. This takes off the edge."

They take turns sipping the hot drink in silence. The calm warmth and the slow cuddle feels so right to him, he's not entirely sure he will ever top this day. That will be a tall order.

"So, what was your favorite part so far?" he asks as he brushes her hair off her forehead and fingers it slowly between his thumb and forefinger.

"Wow. I'm not sure I can pick." She grins deeply. "Plus, it isn't over yet, so I can't make a full assessment yet of a favorite part."

"Fair enough." He sighs. "I'm not sure I can pick one either." He cuddles her body with a double arm squeeze. "What do you want to do tomorrow? We have a free day."

"True. Honestly, I wish the kids could come over. The holidays were so fun with everyone here this year. I want more. If we did a last-minute get-together, and just ordered food, I wonder how many of them could make it?"

"I love that idea. It would be good to see them. Any who could come. I'm not so sure Jaxon could make it, he flies out for work later in the day tomorrow. But maybe the others could." He cocks his head to the side. "Why not try? I'm game."

"Yeah, I agree. Even if only one of them can come."

An easygoing life with her has brought a calmness to Brad's whole self. He can be himself fully with Anna. And she said the same thing to him many times. It's worth more than gold.

"Pinch me," he says with a joking grin.

"Oh, my pleasure!" she says as she proceeds to reach down and pinch his inner thigh.

"Oh, that's how you are going to play it," he declares flirtatiously. "I can play that game." He reaches between her legs and gives her inner thigh a generous squeeze.

She squeals and shifts on his lap. "Eek! But, you missed."

He laughs heartily. "I love you, you know that?"

She nods. "Yes." Her eyes turn lusty. "You love my sex drive."

He raises his eyebrows. "Oh, that's an understatement. And I love all of you. Not just your sex drive. Though I admit I do love that."

She chortles along with him as he tickles his fingers up her thigh, getting ever closer to her slit.

"Mmmm," she murmurs. "And I love yours."

"You going to come lots for your Daddy?"

"Yes, Daddy. I am."

Her eyes are warm pools of lush obedience, full of enjoyment, and twinkling with excitement. And damn, it feels so good to see.

"Good girl." He maneuvers her so he can kiss her. His fingers around her arched neck as they kiss deeply for several minutes, their tongues intertwining. "You taste like toddy."

She spreads her lips into a smile. "So do you. And you are yummy."

The slow build of the day, which had its moments of frantic flurries of mishaps, times of ecstatic elation, and then the crazy follies of the limo, is all the culmination of the ultimate foreplay for the final act of fucking. It was like the build to Christmas or some big event. And to make the big event be their fucking is a triumph Brad happily loves as the orchestrator of the whole thing. There is extraordinary in what is ordinary, if he lives life right.

"I'm going to fuck you hard, babe. I'd love to see my cum dripping from your pussy."

"Mmm, you promise? I love the idea of your cum dripping from my pussy."

"I'll lick it up and make you come again with both of our cum in my mouth."

His cock thickens against her back. This manifestation of his lust for her flares the look of passion in her eyes.

"Someone is ready for the next round." She moves her shoulders so her back rolls against his hard cock. "That thing feels delicious. When do I get it in me?" Her tone entices his lust up a notch higher.

"Soon," he says as he sucks her fingers on her right hand, one by one. He grasps her wettened fingers and nudges them inside her dress to caress her right nipple. Guiding her into self-touch is another joy he relishes frequently. "How's that nipple feel?"

"Hard, wrinkled. And puckered."

"It needs my mouth. I'd better check."

She giggles and swivels to face him, pressing her mound to his engorged penis.

He bares her top half, commandeering her breast and taking her full nipple into his mouth, deep-throating it without any delay. He savors her with his mouth, exploring her nipple as he moans.

Her head falls back as she releases an illicit sigh. "That feels amazing," she coos. "Don't stop."

He works her tit over with his tongue, the hardness of her nipple a delicacy he never tires of. He admits he's basically obsessed with her nipples. Well, he grins, that could be said about her perfect blossom of a pussy too. A flower of ever-changing hues based on her arousal. Another reason to have the lights on during sex is that he gets to observe the changes in her skin color around the mouth of her love canal. A grace he enjoys. His ex never allowed it because she hadn't liked him 'hanging out down there'. With Anna, he savors not only her skin flushing changes, but her feminine aromas, and all on a regular basis because she wants him down there.

"Mmmm, I can smell your arousal," he murmurs against her flesh. "You feel nice and warm now. Are you warmed up?"

"Yes. But I think another round of warm apple crisp sounds amazing. How does it pair with champagne do you think?"

"I think it pairs perfectly." He stands and holds her in his arms, her thighs wrapped around him. He swivels and places her on the couch, snugging a soft throw blanket over her bare chest. "Keep that area nice and toasty while we enjoy it. No need to dress."

She beams up at him. It is a command, but also a request, and one she enjoys submitting to. "Yes, Daddy."

"Let me get it ready, you snuggle up. Don't move." He really enjoys waiting on her, bringing her slippers, glasses of wine, and pampering her to the extreme. She always looks so giddy too, which makes it even more satisfying. Before preparing their second round of dessert, he slips upstairs to check the bath water, which he's sure she's noticed the hum of by now. It's extremely hot. Perfect. He will have plenty of time to carry out his plan of some foreplay pleasure and enjoy dessert with her before the bath water is cooled enough for her to sink into it.

When he returns back downstairs, he stacks a few cheese and cracker piles on a plate, and a small scoop of the apple crisp, and tucks the almost empty champagne bottle under his arm. He gingerly makes his way back to her with the load. The smile she gives him fills his heart with joy and love.

"You look gorgeous, babe, love the cleavage above the blanket." She's so easy to compliment. His ex had often rolled her eyes or given him skeptical looks whenever he complimented her. No matter. She's gone. And good riddance to the bitch.

He hands Anna the plate and the fabric falls off her breasts. "Mmm. That's even better." He settles beside her and takes his first bite. "Scrumptious. You outdid yourself on this crisp."

"More dessert," she says with a giggle. "Well, at least I didn't burn the dessert!" she says with exasperation.

"Yeah, it's so good, babe." He pours them each a half of a glass of champagne.

They clink glasses and take a sip while gazing into each other's eyes.

"I'm gonna fuck you hard, babe. Are you ready?"

Excitement floods her eyes. "Oh, hell yes, I am. I can't wait. I love it when your dominance flares."

"It's been brewing all day. I'm holding back the rage because I have plans. First, I want to bathe you. I want to wash every part of you. Might try to make you come in the bath. Then I'm going to come at you hard, fuck you doggy and make you scream." Being with her had helped him fully realize his own sexuality, which is a gift in its own right. She made him feel like a man more than any woman he'd ever been with.

Her look of anticipation is so satisfying to him. She's as excited for them to have sex as he is, and after this long day of edging, he's ready to let his passion flare as bright as the last time they fucked, which she shared was the hottest sex of her life. He aims to top that.

"I'm burning for you." He gives her an intense look.

"As I'm burning for you," she copies his affirmation. "We can burn together."

They finish their small snack, and he pulls her back on his lap. Instantly, his semi thickens against her backside. He nuzzles her from behind as she squirms in the hold of his body and arms around her. He strokes her cheeks, then starts to touch her arms, following the concentric circle idea of slowly arousing her from the outside in, starting at her limbs where he will caress her ever closer to her core, touching her pussy last. He never understood those men who went straight for pussy. They missed out on so much sensuousness with their women. He'd been no dummy as an adult man. Even now in his fifties, he knew he could still improve his lovemaking skills, and he made the effort to. He'd read several books on female arousal when he'd met Anna. With her being so open to expanding her sexuality, he wanted to live out that part of their life together to the maximum. It had proved to be the best thing he could have done for their marriage, better than any monetary prep, smarter than any move he could have dreamt up. And then she had taught him her body, her reactions, and the result had been more glorious than he'd thought possible. But it all only happened because he paid very close attention to every nuance, every slight change of her expressions, and her instinctual reactions to what he did. She'd allowed him to take control and it freed her up to react naturally.

She caresses his thighs and leans her head against his chest. "You are so warm and comfy."

"Don't forget horny," he says with a chuckle. "I can feel the devil on my shoulder already." He titters a laugh. "Lots of devils, in fact."

"Mmmm, I love that devil on your shoulder. It always means I get another orgasm, or ten." She giggles, which turns into a low appreciative hum as he caresses her skin. "You always make me feel so amazing, Brad."

"You are my priority, babe. Always."

Chapter 3

Anna

He never has to say it, it's always evident, but it feels so lovely to hear him say it. Being a man's 'priority' was new to Anna upon meeting Brad. It felt awkward at first. She was no damn diva. She was an independent, strong woman. But he had taught her that didn't mean she couldn't be taken care of. In fact, he had told her when they first started dating that he loved her independent spirit and strong will. It had taken time for her to realize that his taking care of her didn't mean she was weak or incapable of it herself. It was something entirely different. And she found she loved it.

He drags his fingers lightly over her body, cresting the mounds of her breasts, the stiffening peaks of her nipples, all the curves of her torso get visited by his meandering fingertips. He palms both her hips before taking a dive down her thighs to her knees, then back up. His patterns show he understands so well that seduction begins way before actual foreplay. And it works damn well on her.

"Please," she begs.

He releases a sigh and presses his fingers to her mons pubis. He swirls his fingers around her fleshy mound, then massages it deeper.

"Please, more," she slurs, getting more ravenous for his cock by the second.

He lifts the hem of her dress and pushes two fingers into her clit, then drags them down her slit, and continues to repeat the move.

"You are really wet," he whispers.

"Of course, you've worked me into a frothy, wanton wench with all this play. I just want your cock in me." Her kitty throbs with pulsations of desire. She's ready to hop up and try to tackle him. She knows he'd get a kick out of that as surely as she knows she'd fail miserably at taking him down, until he acquiesced willingly. She recalls a day just before Christmas when she'd

143

done just that, and he'd laughed in delight and let her take him down. The sex afterward in front of the lit Christmas tree had been incredible.

"I can manage that. Just a taste of it, though." He wiggles his body so he can penetrate her pussy from beneath her.

She groans as he easily sinks his fingers into her warm, wet slit.

He lines up his cockhead at her hole and sinks himself into her. He groans out profusely at the first full penile penetration of her pussy.

"Mmmm fuck yesss," she mumbles in agreement. "Fuck me, Daddy," she whimpers out, expressing how extremely wanton she is for more of his cock.

He does a small circle around the head of her itty bitty clit as he thrusts up into her. She loves that he knows right where to touch her clitoral head and with what pressure to drive her insane with want. Next, he slides his fingers down from her bean and rolls the shaft of her clit. She moans her happiness with his touch.

"Oh, my Gawd yes." Her panting increases as he gently pumps himself into her. "I could come, I'm so turned on."

He's breathing rapidly while back at working her clit vigorously. "I could too," he says in a strained voice. He immediately pulls his cock out of her with a deep grunt. "Fuck."

She whines. "What? You are stopping? No," she purrs in an exaggerated 'O'.

"Whew. I had to stop. Bath first." He's panting heavily.

"Then let's get my ass in that tub." She reluctantly stands up and instantly regrets it. "I should have stayed there on you. You'd have come, wouldn't you?"

He nods, looking a bit strained. "Yeah, I almost did. Barely stopped it."

"Damnit!" she shouts with a stomp. "Why do I always get you uber close, then you get a pass?"

He chuckles. "I'm pretty sure I did that to myself." He shakes his head. "I'm in control. And trust me, I want to come more than you want me to."

"Hardly. I doubt that." She pouts.

He rises off the couch and scoops her hand in his. "Let's go fuck."

"You mean, let's go take a bath." She sighs heavily. "There's no fuck in the word bath."

"No, I mean let's go fuck. The bath is a part of the fuck, babe."

"Okay, if you say so." She's skeptical, and that's a stretch. Okay. It's not. She knows he's right. She's just monstrously impatient for his cock.

Once upstairs, Anna scans the room. On the bed, she notices her new harness is laid out. "Is that my fucking attire?"

"Yes. I've been dreaming of controlling your body in that thing in a doggy fuck for weeks. I'm not dissing that dream." His facial smirk is cute. "I love that 'fucking attire', that's exactly right."

Her desire for him to fuck her doggy was always pretty strong. And his wants match her on that front. She loves it when he loses control in a rage fuck and pounds her rapidly, especially when he fucks her head down into the mattress. She knows many women who hate the jackhammer sex, but she loves it, especially when she's wet and so aroused she's begging for his cock inside her. It's all a grind and she loves the full gradient of it. He is so good at getting her to that hyper-aroused state. A master at it, really. There is a time for a sweet slow lovemaking, and a time for wild abandon. She always desired both types from Brad. She'd feared this stage of her life because she'd heard many women disliked sex in midlife, but she also realized most of them were likely just bored with the sex they were having or weren't being stimulated properly enough to enjoy it.

Neither is the case with Brad.

He's a gem. She smiles. Her man can fix any broken thing she gives him—it's certainly not her forte to fix things. He could cook up a culinary masterpiece of a meal and can grow veggies like no one else she knows. Plus, he prioritizes her constantly, not that she asked him to, but he chooses to. He helps clean the house, does laundry without her asking, and wants to spend his spare time with her. She couldn't imagine a better husband if she'd read about him in a romance novel. Her life is a romance novel, but better, it's an erotic romance because Brad is always horny as fuck and yearns to make her climax. It's complete bliss! She knows there will come a time when she gets pissed at him, that's reality, but she also knows it will be a different resolution than she's ever had in a relationship. She has that much faith in them. Her smugness feels truthful and being able to gloat about a good relationship feels so damn good.

She grins. "I can't wait for you to pull me into doggy position by those straps. It's making my pussy flare right now just thinking about it." She'd felt her hole flaring before in her past life during arousal, but never as much as she enjoys her body doing it with Brad by her side. Dude is a magic fucker. Sex is magic and he'd figured it out.

He guides her to the bathtub with an excited expression. It's warm in the bathroom, the candles are flickering, the scents are lush and soothing. "Wow. This is a dream, Brad." The other thing about them is neither of them had ever had any partner who appreciated them as much as they appreciated each other. And that made all the difference.

"You deserve to be pampered. I'm going to bathe you. I want you to just lay there and relax." He caresses her face. "I want to wash you."

She nods as he leads her to step into the water, her stomach swirling all aflame with his promises. The bathwater is warm, on the verge of hot, so it's ideal.

"Oh, wow. That feels amazing," she says as she sinks fully into the water, noting how it drains her fully of the memory of the shivers from earlier. She has no stress, zero worries, and only pleasure bodes near her. She'd never allowed a lover this much intimacy before to bathe her, but no lover of hers had ever asked to bathe her either, or pampered her this much. Brad had admitted to her he'd read books on how to seduce women, which made her smile. She loves that he is a sex nerd, because she is too. She ends up relishing his catering to all her needs, wants, and desires rather than caring where his ideas came from in the first place. Who the fuck cares if he got it from a book? Back when she had been on personal talking terms with her sister, she'd shared that with her about Brad. All she'd done was put him down, stating he had no original ideas. Seriously? And she was so wrong. Thinking back, she wishes she'd told her sister to shut her pie hole and walked out. Jealousy is extra ugly when it's on a family member's face. She shuts that down, stops thinking about her now.

The first time Brad asked to bathe her, she had been taken aback. Washing oneself is a very personal intimate act, and to allow another to do it was an effort. She had to learn to be patient and just allow him to do all the things at his own pace because he liked to touch her. She knew she could do it more efficiently and quicker, but that wasn't the point. The thing was she found he wanted to savor her. It had been almost a startling experience the very first time he brushed a washcloth along her flesh, but she figured out how to sink into it herself and baste in his caretaking, sort of marinating in his affections for her. He liked to 'do' for her and being a major doer in her last marriage had brought this type of act to the front door of her intimate comfort level.

Having been with her ex who just barged in because he considered it his right had been unnerving to Anna, leaving her feeling uncomfortable all the time, wondering when he'd barge in again. His lack of respect for her privacy had caused her to clam up, to avoid doing certain things while he was around, and to generally fit her needs in around where he happened to be each moment. She had realized one day she lived constantly on edge. She got lost in the inability to prioritize her own needs. It had forced her to live in the moment so much so that planning never worked out. She'd had to seize her moments of freedom and alone time like a miser. But it was all so different with Brad, he glorified in her needs. And though she'd taken to his openness and nonjudgmental ways immediately, it had been like going from breathing syrup for air to daily imbibing the loveliest, calmest, freshest ocean-scented breeze. The real-life living experience difference between the two men is night and day.

"You look deep in thought," he whispers as he dips the washcloth in the water.

She cringes, not wanting to admit her thoughts, so she asks, "What did I do to deserve such a devoted husband?"

He chuckles softly as he lifts her arm and rubs the soapy washcloth over it. "You deserve all my devotion and more. You are the smartest, most beautiful, amazing, fearless, and empowered woman I know."

She sighs loving the caresses his words are delivering upon her soul. "And a lot of that has to do with you, Brad."

"You did it, not me. I can't take credit for who you are."

"You did do it. Your support has brought me all the way to this point. Without you, I wouldn't be how I am, or who I am."

"You've always been you."

He might have her there, but there's no denying that he's played a gargantuan role in her growth. "Look at me, Brad." A lump forms in her throat and she is overcome with the urge to cry. In a shaky voice, she says, "When I think about who I was before I walked into that bookstore, I was a shell of who I am now. And it terrifies me to think about the fact that our meeting was so accidental that we almost didn't meet."

"We were meant to be, babe. You're my soul mate. If it hadn't happened then, I believe it would have happened another way at another time." He seems confident of that, but all she feels is the shadow of the fear that they may have never met. She shudders despite the warm water.

He presses his lips to her lips and holds her cheeks. Then he kisses her nose, her forehead, and over each closed eyelid. "We would have met, babe. Even if I would have had one day only with you, you are worth waiting a lifetime for."

Tears bleep out of her eyes and both relief and joy fill her at once as he pulls her out of the tub partially to hold her.

"Aw, babe. It's okay." He caresses her back as her sobs flare then wane. "You're the best lover, wife, and best friend I could have ever hoped for."

She nods excessively. "Same. Same, Brad. So much so." She sinks back into the tub and sighs. "Sorry, I lost it."

"Don't you ever apologize for feeling amazing about us. I love that you were overcome with emotion. It shows me how much you love me. How close we've become."

"Awww, my turn to say that." His use of the words 'best friend' rolls about inside her. It's true, they are, but she hadn't thought of them as that until just now. But it fit so succinctly that she wonders how she never thought of their relationship that way before. She is always thinking of them as partners, spouses, the masculine and the feminine energies, the yin and the yang, but they are so much more, and best friends really rounds it out perfectly.

She smiles through her tear-stained cheeks, her vulnerability on display for him without a single worry or care, and says, "I got you all wet."

"That's my line," he snickers with a devilish grin.

"I'm glad that's out of the way. I bet it's the hot toddy and the champagne."

"I bet it's just your heart feeling, babe." He gently scrubs the washcloth on the base of her throat, then travels down her upper chest in slow circles. "Let yourself feel, honey, and I love that you shared. It brings us even closer."

She grins at his use of 'honey', which he saves for only certain times. Her playful streak now raises its head. "I'd rather you feel me." She gives him all the passion she has for him in her gaze, as much as she can pack in.

"Oof, if that look doesn't say 'Take me, Daddy' I've never seen one! Rawr!" he mutters gruffly.

He drags the soft cloth along her breasts and traces the edge of her right areola. His gentle touch after the masculine growl is intoxicating. His eyes are on her face as he increases the pressure of his fingers on her nipple. He encases the hard tip of her tit in the warm wet cloth and pinches it, then gives it a little tug. "I love love love your nip wrinkles."

"Mmmmm," she murmurs, writhing in the water, making it splash up the sides of the tub. "That feels so damn good." He'd taught her the value of a washcloth as a sex toy over the many baths he'd given her. She savors how sexually imaginative he is and how lucky she is because of it.

"You are so sexy, fuck, I love touching you like this and looking at your body in the water. You really are so beautiful, honey."

She's gifted the 'honey' once more. "You make me feel like no other person on Earth ever has," she says in a low luxurious voice.

"Same." He massages the washcloth along her tummy, skates quickly past her crotch with a big grin as he mutters, "Later." He tickles the cloth along the tops of her thighs before washing both legs and feet, taking extra time to gently swipe the washcloth between each of her painted toes.

He motions for her to roll to her side and begins to scrub her back with the soapy cloth, not skipping her neck or shoulders before dragging it down her spine to her buttocks. "Can't forget your cute little butt."

He rubs in a circular motion around both her butt cheeks, then dives into the crevice of her ass to lightly buff her anus. Her boundary is external anal play only, and he has never ever crossed that, not even a tiny push. She's always loved his respect for her wishes and hard stops, and he has never made her feel less than because of them. This is new ground to be able to have this much trust in another human being, and it has brought them to a new place. It's delivered to them the fullness that absolute intimacy offers, before Brad, she didn't even understand full intimacy. It isn't just a state of mind, it's now a way of life.

She twerks a little against his touch, enjoying the rub for a few minutes before he presses her hip for her to situate herself flat again. Being cared for this indulgently always makes her feel raw. That vulnerability is an opening of a flower bud, allowing him to thoroughly love the most intimate parts of her, and not just of her body. And that love always includes him stimulating her to her highest sexual peaks.

"It's later," he whispers pulling the cloth along her hip, making his way toward the private space between her thighs. He presses his washcloth-wrapped fingers to her slit and rides it up and down gently. When he focuses on rubbing her clit, she sighs.

"Mmmmmm, I think I love 'later,'" she murmurs as her eyes fall closed.

"Ditto," he says in a whisper. "Babe, I'm going to make you come in the bath. Then we will move to the bed." He clears his throat. "I'll wash your hair in the morning in the shower, okay? I don't want to take time on that. I want you."

"Yes," she says in a barely audible voice. The warmth of the water, the light sheen of the candles across the bathroom, Brad's sexy voice, and his arousing touch have taken her to a dreamlike state. She is lingering near climax already.

"I'm not holding back. I'm coming in hot," he says in his stern, masculine voice. He turns on the rose clitoral sucker toy, the hum increasing to the third power.

She smiles through half-closed eyes. "You know."

He submerges the toy and nods as he spreads the cleft of her pussy lips to reveal her clitoral head. Then he firmly presses the mouth of it to her flesh.

She cries out in deep pleasure immediately, the touchdown of the toy launching her almost the rest of the way up her climax climb. "Oh, fuck," she whispers with a body twitch. She squirms in the water, moving to absorb as much of the toy's vibrations against her sensitive clit as she can. She wants to beg to come but can't seem to speak.

Brad grabs her left nipple and manipulates it between his fingertips, then he does the same on her right nip. The more aggressive he molests her nipples, the more she moans.

"Do you want to come, babe?"

She nods, speech is becoming ever more difficult.

"Hold off a tiny bit more to build. You can do it. I'm right here."

She grunts impatience as she fights the wave of her orgasm. Her clitoris wants to crash. She rolls her body to try to garner control, but it slips out of her grasp. She becomes gripped with desperation. A whimper squeak slips out of her mouth. "Daddy," she pleads. "Please."

"Come for me, baby. Give it to me. Submit to me. Come for your Daddy."

Hearing him always brings her to a climax. She relishes waiting for him to command her to release. At the magic words, she relinquishes her hold over her edging and the floodgates of her orgasm burst her pleasure free. She exclaims loudly as the contractions reverberate inside her, causing ripples throughout her whole body. Her back arches. Her head dips back into the water. Her legs straighten and tense, raise up off the floor of the tub. Her body twitches as she is delivered into a second peak of the orgasm. She gasps out deeply after having held her breath. She'd read how a woman shouldn't hold her breath while orgasming, but it is proving hard for her to break the habit.

"Oh, fuck yes, babe. That was a big one. I love this. Makes my cock so hard."

"Double," she whispers.

"Beautiful! I love it." He removes the toy from contact with her bean. "Okay, now float down."

She opens her eyes in a series of rapid fluttering of her eyelids. "Wow."

"Wow is right," he says with clear enjoyment. "I got a wow."

"Wow. Wow. Wow," she musters out quietly.

"I got four wows!" he says triumphantly.

She smiles as he holds her cheek, gazes into her eyes, then caresses his hand down her torso and back up again.

"That looked pretty epic and huge."

"Oh, it was. It was incredible." She rolls her shoulders savoring the water cradling her as she comes down off the orgasmic high.

"You're incredible."

"No, you are."

"Time to dry off and get you coated in massage oil." He reaches for her hand to help her step out of the tub.

"Oh, that's the next stage, huh?"

"Yup. This is full-blown pampering, before hardcore fucking."

An explosion of excited anticipation bursts inside her gut. "Oh, my gosh. I literally cannot wait!" She needs his cock in her. The orgasm helped, but it's not his cock in her pussy.

He cradles her arm as he helps her to the stand on the tile floor. They connect their gazes. Both of them smile.

She fully shows him all she's feeling via her eyes, she doesn't need to shield any part of herself from him. This global freedom is what had fully healed her and made her his, which he only wanted because she had fully granted it. The flow of it had to be two-way and not hindered by anything. No shadows of wrongdoing, no need for forgiveness, no bad feelings to create doubt. It is the nirvana of their unconditional and full love. That he could love her yet fuck her hard brought all her wants and desires together in a full world of pleasure that could only have come from Brad.

With warm loving, appreciative eyes, he dries her body off. Sniffing along her skin, he sighs. "Mmmm, you smell delicious." He caresses her breasts. "And your skin is so moist and soft." He scoops her up and carries her like a baby to the bed. He lays her across it, then reaches for the oil.

"Wow, you are unbelievable. I get a massage now too?" Her tone is incredulous, but this is so much of a Brad move. She knows full well what a back massage usually leads to with Brad, and she's grinning big with her cheek nestled up against the comforter.

"Oh, yes, for sure you do."

Chapter 4
Brad

Hovering above her back, his hard cock trails her buttocks as he nibbles her ear. She squeals and wiggles beneath him. Her warm water-soaked skin pressed to his raises his lust to the max, he wants so badly to ram himself inside her and explode. Precum seeps out of his cockhead, drawing his juices in a meandering sprawl upon her naked flesh as he moves—like a river on a map. His mouth travels in kisses along her neck, shoulder blades, and on down to her ass.

"My princess, my good girl, my lover, my partner, my wife, my slut, and my whore." His voice is getting extra growly with the dirty words.

She coos appreciatively with each of his declarations, her body trembling.

"Yes," she says with a larger quiver.

He smiles. "Make your clit twitch?"

She nods. "Mmm hmmm."

He loves her in the full gamut of those labels, and beyond any labels, despite them, and because of them. But he enjoys saying each in the right moment, mood, and situation dependent, yet she's all of them at once now. A beautiful, kind, loving, smart woman who also loves sex and dirty talk. What more could he possibly want for more than just more of her? Allowing her to fully realize her own sexuality has been such a rewarding journey, and his has flourished right alongside hers. Granted, she had more past shit to overcome than he did, but he is constantly honored and astounded by the level of trust she awards him. Maybe that's part of why it is so easy for her to trust him fully.

His inner dominance is flaring, and he aggressively reigns himself in. He needs to slow his libido down a bit, own that control he so loves to exert upon her. First, fully pampering her to the point of so much relaxation she almost falls asleep, but with full seduction mode intertwined. He wants her begging for his cock inside her again, and then this time, he gets to deliver. It definitely needs to be sex after...the full buildup...the most exquisite connection...the most wanton anticipation.

He hadn't fully realized the range of his dominant side until he had been living with Anna. It had raged while they dated, but being by her side in the same house he has really had the chance to allow it to flourish, but not without her grace. And the beautiful thing has been that as he had grown more dominant, she'd embraced more submission. They were able to dance that ancient phenomenon, that baring of their souls because they had both been open to it. Not just that, they indulged in it. As natural as the act of sex itself, their relationship is the expanse that nature is, encompassing the feminine and masculine energies so wondrously entwined, and in all its glory too.

"I'm going to fuck you like a rag doll, drag you across the bed by the straps of that harness on you, and fuck you doggy like a slut whore wench."

She shudders beneath him, then twitters, "Yes, please, Daddy." She has admitted to him that she delights in his commanding demeanor, and even the brute strength he has over her.

He can smell her arousal peaking, that loss of control he yearns for in her at his will, just as his has been contained for the moment. He squirts the oil across her skin and begins to work it in. With every shred of his senses on overload, he carefully massages her muscles, not too hard, not too soft. He can wait to satiate his desires.

"You going to be my good girl?"

The automatic phrase slips out of her mouth again. "Yes, Daddy."

"Then after I fuck you, I want to paint your tits in my cum, smear it around, then lick and suck my salty cum off." He knows he has too many plans, but he also knows hearing what he wants to do to her ticks her passion higher.

He works the muscles in her back, her biceps, and arms, then spends a good amount of time on her buttocks, then thighs, shins, and feet. He climbs up her body and lays upon her, pressing his steel rod hard cock against her back. He breathes heavily in her ear as he massages her temples. She mewls softly acknowledging and appearing to soak up all of his touches. He straddles her, his taint pressed to her flesh, and runs his hands around her scalp.

"Damn, that feels so good. And I love it when you straddle me like this. I can feel the warmth at the base of your cock."

"Time for her massage." He crawls backward and slides his right hand between her legs. Her pussy lips are slick and thick. "Mmmm, you are wet. Swollen."

"Yes, I am. Because of you. I want you to fuck me." She squirms. "I want your cock, Daddy."

"Soon," he says and shushes her start of further protest. "You are coming again first," he commands. He props her middle up on the wedge sex pillow and dives into her pussy with his mouth open. He indulges his passion a bit as he hoovers her lady bits into his mouth and aggressively sucks while finger fucking her with two fingers. With his mouth jammed to her clit as a full-blown latch on, he sucks her as hard as he can.

She writhes, moans, screams out, then comes quickly within two minutes flat.

He'd mastered that move last month and he'd used it frequently on her since. It is so effective. The only other thing that quickens her climax is when he adds in nipple action, which he laments not doing now cause it is one of his favorite things to do to her.

"Oh, my Gawd, fuck," she pants out between gasps, sounding spent already. "Holy fuck that drives me crazy."

Brad loosens his hold a bit further on his beastly passion, but just a little bit. Not too much. He scoots back, grabs her by the ankles, and drags her across the bed.

She squeals in delight, pretending to claw the blanket in protest.

He tugs her harder until she is resting at the edge as if he'd bent her over it. He resists the strong temptation to penetrate her and manages to pull her to stand. He plants a multitude of kisses along the back of her neck. Her hands meander up his face and tangle in his hair.

"I want you, Daddy."

"I want you. Be my slut." His urge to ravage her is near peak threshold. Loss of containment is imminent.

"I am, Daddy. I'm your slut," she murmurs.

That pushes him clean over the edge. He bends her over quickly, which releases a toot out her bunghole.

She curls into a ball laughing on the bed as Brad busts a gut along with her.

"You pushed the wrong button," she cries out between her hysterical laughter. "Oh, my Gawd! I've never farted in front of you before!"

He doubles over with a guffaw. She looks so cute and sweet, yet still so sexy.

"Oh, damn. That was too funny," he guffaws.

"Well, my damn ass ruined the moment." Her laughing subsides as he gathers up the harness in his palm.

"Not ruined at all, baby." He smirks. "Our bodies make sounds."

"I might as well round it out and belch now," she jokes.

He laughs with her, but his level of horny has not waned one single bit. No fart in the world could stop his lust for her.

She straightens her body as a last bit of laughter peels out of her lungs and he helps her to stand. Her little smile is humble and amusing. She bites her lip.

"I'm ready," she murmurs. "Daddy."

Her saying 'Daddy' to him always rages him up inside. Add in her nakedness and it's a feast for his senses as he fits the straps of the harness to her torso and hips. He takes his time savoring her curves and thoughts of him doggy fucking her consume his brain. He quickly swivels her to face away from him. He bends her over the bed's edge quickly and she chuckles. "Apparently nothing loaded in the chamber this time."

He mirrors her chuckle, then caresses her body, enjoying the road bumps the straps offer along her smooth flesh.

She groans out, "Mmm, yes." She sighs her lovely feminine sigh. "Even after all you've been touching me, I can't get enough."

He loves her confession. "Same, baby, I can't get enough of you."

Seeing her bent over in front of him, her holes on display, he relishes his imminent mounting of her, entering her body, and rocking it from behind. He roughly grasps the straps framing her hips and pulls her to a hands-and-knees position on the bed. He wants to see her tits hang like petals and rock back and forth quickly as he fucks her.

"Yes, head down, ass up. Wanting to watch your tits swing, babe." He grips the leather with one hand and spanks her ass with his dick with the other.

She shakes her bum. "Please, Daddy, I want you in me."

Her pleading churns him up more. He lifts the cage off his passion and penetrates her pussy with the head of his engorged hardon. He progresses rapidly to hard and fast thrusts and fucks her like an animal.

Her grunts are almost as primal as his as he fucks her hard, slapping himself against her body violently, making her butt cheeks gyrate, and her tits swing fast.

"Fuck," he mutters almost coming already. He forces himself to slow down and rides her hole slower. This allows him to catch his breath a bit. He's not coming yet. No way. He captures her hips and slow fucks her for several minutes, cherishing the feel of her pussy encasing his aroused penis.

Raging again, he snatches up the harness and orders, "Head down, ass up."

She's slow to respond so he presses her head to the bed, taking great pleasure in dominating her. He tugs on the straps, even though she's on her knees to assert his power, and her submission.

She purrs obedience and stays put where he placed her.

"Good girl," he says roughly, but with approval.

He begins a rapid pounding of her in an animalistic fuck. He doesn't hold back, but fucks her like a wild beast.

Chapter 5

Anna

"Oh, yes, oh my Gawd," she pants. She peels out an impatient grunt, close to climaxing again because she loves him fucking her this way with wild abandon. At one point in her life, she had found doggy fucking embarrassing. She hadn't enjoyed her partner staring at her in such a vulnerable way, nor the suggestion of free access to her, plus, she just hadn't enjoyed it with him. Period. But that was due to the nature of their bad marriage. She'd enjoyed it in her youth, but things had switched due to regretful reasons she decided right now was not the time to revisit.

She concentrates on how it feels to have him slam against her bottom, to take his pleasure from her body in the way only a pussy can provide. She loves making Brad come and she senses he's close to the taste of victory. She smirks against the soft blanket. It might be her taste of victory. Either way, after the day of play they'd had, victory would be well deserved.

"Whose cum do you want dripping out of your pussy?" he demands.

"Yours, Daddy."

"Who's your Dom?"

"You, Daddy."

He tugs the straps firmly.

She is loving the control he has over her body with the harness. At first, she just thought it was a sexy thing to wear, but now she gets that it's such a tool of dominance that it's massively yummy. He's not shirking his use of the control either, to her utter delight. He grabs the straps across her back and uses them for more leverage to ram his cock into her, then he grapples the straps across her hips and continues to fuck her roughly, just how she's told him she loves. She can't get enough. This harness is certainly topping her favorite in their collection of sex toys. Their juices make sloshing sounds as he slides in and out of her vagina. He gives her clit a fast rub; she moans in pleasure ready to launch again.

He claims her straps once more, growls like he's close to climaxing, then he smashes himself into her so fast and hard she knows he's likely coming in mere seconds.

Finally.

She notices extra fluid inside her as he begins to slow down his barrage of her cunt. She smiles, knowing she was right. He came and he came hard.

"Fuck," he spews, still feeding his cock into her on repeat, fucking his seed back into her. "Holy fuck. Wow! Whew! That was a selfish fuck."

"Oh, no. I loved it," she coos. He is not even remotely selfish. "I love that you got yours. I love it when you come."

"I'm still hard." He hands her a clit pen toy. "Your turn again." He continues to pump into her.

She presses the toy on the high level and holds it on her clit. She's so aroused, she will come quickly. His using her body to come turns her on, but she's also turned on when he puts her first. It's everything to get both from him, but in a way that respects her, that highlights her pleasure. He always says, 'I know I will come. That's a given.'

He takes over control of the toy. "Just relax, babe, I want to make you come again."

His wanting to take care of the toy and make her come again is a giant turn-on by itself. She plunges immediately into another delicious big O.

He proceeds to bring her to climax twenty-two more times. Well, at her best count. She's so cum drunk from climaxing, she's not exactly sure. But one thing she does know, she is the biggest winner.

Brad climaxes once more as well, and they crumple in a heap tangled together on the bed.

"You won."

"You won."

They both erupt into laughter.

"Best day ever, Brad."

"Who?" he inquires with a smile and stern gaze.

"Daddy," she slurs happily.

"My good girl."

They hold each other, resting for about ten minutes before Brad rises. "Nearing the final phase."

She cocks her head. What could that be?

Chapter 6
Brad

"Lay on your tummy."

"I think we've used just about every sex toy we own, at least once."

"It's not a sex toy. I want to make you feel amazing."

"I already do feel amazing. Like exhilarated. So alive. I'm soaring!"

He grins. "On your tummy, babe. Submit to me."

She obeys. "Okay, if you say so." She snuggles into the soft bed on her belly, enjoying the flood of endorphins swimming inside her.

He squirts the oil along her back in a crisscross pattern and begins to give her another massage.

"Wow, this is positively luxurious. I'm a queen of queens."

"Yes, you are. Thank you for that. I was so pent up and I was really enjoying fucking you hard." He's often told her he's afraid he might go too far and not be able to control himself.

"Oh, as did I. I absolutely loved it. I lost count, but I think it was in the twenties."

"Yeah, that's my guess too. I think twenty-four." He chortles. "You are amazing. A goddess of sex. I'm so proud of you."

"Only because you've helped me realize all this about my body. It's also because of you."

He continues to massage her back, maybe he should take credit too, but it is her who has opened up to it all. He's just the lucky one who gets to be with her. "I'm the luckiest man in the world."

"I'm the luckiest," she retorts in a positive tone.

He spends extra time on her lower back and buttocks, then her thighs. After a ten-minute massage, during which he fears she may have already fallen asleep, he nudges her. "Lay on my lap, babe." He situates himself against the back pillow at the headboard and pats his lap.

She crawls lazily up the bed and places her head on him.

He strokes her hair. "I'm so proud of you. I can't express it enough. Whenever we try something new, I get so turned on and excited when it works. When it works, that is. Like today. And the harness works for you too, right?"

"Oh, my goodness, yes! It's unbelievable. I love how at your slightest whim you can mold my body. It's extraordinarily hot to have you have that much control over my body. This is the best purchase ever! Aside from my clit toys."

He gives a short belly laugh. "Yeah, well those are unbeatable."

"True."

He continues to play with her hair, hoping she will fall asleep in his lap.

"So, tomorrow will be fun. Can't wait to check our phones and see which kids can come." She yawns.

He twirls a curl between his fingers, then brushes her locks on repeat with his open hand. "Yes, it will be fun to see whoever can make it. What should we make for food?"

"Well, I'm sure as fuck making that damn cheese sauce. I will triumph over that loss. Then whatever else, I'm game. We can decide in the morning. It seems like too much effort to decide much of a menu now." She yawns again as he rubs her back.

"You were amazing."

"No, you were amazing. No one has ever made me feel the way you do." She yawns again. She's getting close. "Maybe I can make that cheese brie appetizer with berry preserves I made at New Year's. That was so good."

"Yeah, that would be perfect. I could grill, I guess. Ribs, perhaps?"

"It's so cold, are you sure you want to do something long like that? How about chicken wings?"

"Yeah, that works. I'd be outside shorter. Though I turn them frequently, overall, the time outside is likely a bit shorter. We can hit the grocery store and see what they have for meat. Decide then."

She cackles. "Toy or no toy this time?"

He releases a light chuckle. "Well, now that is a good question. Either way, I'll find time to pleasure you tomorrow too. Every day, babe, every day."

"I love you," she blurts out. "So very much. And I think our love won't grow. But then it does."

"I feel the same way, babe." He brushes his hand along her soft cheek, loving the sleepy dreamy look on her face. "I will love you for eternity."

She snuggles her head against his lap. She's silent for several moments, he wonders if she conked out, but she speaks again in a very weak voice, "Brad, I feel so incredible, I just can't tell you ..." she trails off and falls completely silent. Her even breathing tells Brad she's fallen asleep.

He smiles deeply, enjoying that he's made her feel so sexually satisfied, comfortable, and relaxed that she just falls asleep in his lap. Thoughts flood his brain. He really railed her hard tonight. Her moans were off the charts, though, so he surmises she was honest when she said she loved it. He fucked her with so much force, and yet he feels like he's loved her like a delicate flower in the tender moments of the evening. He caresses her hair a few more times as he watches her sleep deepen. His smile doesn't wane in the passing minutes. Today was a treasure, a day of extreme sexual play neither of them will ever forget. A day that he will cherish. No matter what comes, he will have these memories.

He is a satisfied Dom. She is his satiated sub. The day was perfect, even with all the crazy mishaps. His eyelids are heavy as he glances at the clock. Bed at 9:49 pm. Wow. An early night. Even if he can't ever come up with a better idea to top this day, it won't matter because it was a day that topped even his wildest dreams. And it couldn't have happened with anyone else the way it happened with Anna. His eyes fall closed as he gazes down at his sleeping wife.

The End

About the Author

RUAN WILLOW IS AN EROTICA author, sex blogger at https://ruanwillowauthor.com/ , sexuality and erotica fiction podcaster at the Oh F*ck Yeah with Ruan Willow Podcast[1] , and an audiobook narrator/voiceover actor. She is also published on Medium https://medium.com/@ruanwillow, Frolic Me, and Literotica. She loves spending time with family and friends, interacting with fans, cooking, sharing/chatting with and educating people about sex, reading, travel, being outdoors, swimming, learning about sex, podcasting, and more sex. Did you catch all the sex? She's giggling right now thinking about you reading all about sex. She values openness and talking about the natural act of sex. And. Yup, she loves to laugh!

---

1. https://ohfckyeahwithruanwillow.buzzsprout.com/

Thank you!

Thank you to all my family and friends who support me. I wouldn't be where I am without you. You are all the magic and the light in my life, the love that grows in my love. I am honestly thrilled and humbled by the supportive people in my life. Love you!

To Fans:

Thank you for purchasing and/or reviewing this book!

I peddle fantasies for the purposes of your enjoyment, entertainment, and expanding your sexuality and openness. Always remember that no fantasies are bad. You should enjoy your sexuality and your fantasy life as much and as often as you can.

Thank you for reading my book! I write for myself and for my fans. My fans are my main focus though, but of course, I want to like what I write too, and I thoroughly enjoyed writing these stories.

In writing erotica/erotic romance, I'm always excited for the erotic journey! I'm on a path of sexual empowerment, enlightenment, and enjoyment. Thank you for reading this and I'm honored to be a part of your journey as well.

I am where I am because fans have responded to me and my content, so I owe everything to you! Thank you! Thank you! Thank you! You are a blessing in my life, and you give me more joy than you will ever know. I love interacting with all of you and I will never give that up.

My stories are erotica, so they have a generous amount of sex in them, as I believe our relationships should have as well. I hope you enjoyed this novella for what it is, literature that is in the erotica genre. It is very different from the romance genre, and there are different levels of heat in the erotica genre as well. Explore them all!

If you'd like more of my work, please see below for my list of published works on the following pages, visit my sexuality and erotica podcast, find my audiobooks, visit my website, my Patreon, visit my profile on Medium, and my linktree with all my links at https://linktr.ee/RuanWillow

Thank you for purchasing this book, I'd love to hear your thoughts in an honest review on the site where you purchased the book from. I'd absolutely love it if you shared my book with others. It warms my heart profusely when I see someone who has taken the time to review/share my book. Love you all very much!

All my best, yours truly, with overflowing love from a full heart,
Ruan Willow
Erotica author, sexuality/erotica podcaster, and erotic book narrator
Ruan's books and audiobooks: https://books.ruanwillowauthor.com/
All Ruan's links in one spot: Ruan's links[2]

2.   https://linktr.ee/RuanWillow

Oh F*ck Yeah with Ruan Willow Podcast

It's free on podcast apps! Also airing on the internet radio station Full Swap Radio website and app Tuesdays and 6 pm CST, and Wednesdays 8 am (subject to change, check for the current schedule online) AND the PodNation TV Network/Roku TV/Fire TV powered by Podnation Pods anytime VOD on the app, and Sundays and Mondays After Dark Hours around 11 pm Eastern Time Zone (subject to change), watch it here: player frontlayer https://player.frontlayer.com/live/fl427618

Oh F*ck Yeah with Ruan Willow Podcast on Buzzsprout[1]

Join the exclusive level of the podcast for $3 a month: https://www.buzzsprout.com/1599808/subscribe

Podcast link to Apple Podcasts Oh F*ck Yeah with Ruan Willow on Apple[2]

Podcast link to Spotify (check out Ruan's public playlists on Spotify where the episodes are categorized by topic) Oh F*ck Yeah with Ruan Willow Podcast on Spotify[3]

---

1.   https://ohfckyeahwithruanwillow.buzzsprout.com/

2.   https://podcasts.apple.com/us/podcast/oh-f-ck-yeah-with-ruan-willow/id1550869095

3.   https://open.spotify.com/show/1rmfiA8FVPG766ouQ9P3QG

Ruan's other books and novellas: https://books.ruanwillowauthor.com/

Decadent Erotica, An Anthology

3rd Place Winner in the 2022 Golden Pigtails Smut Awards for Dark/ Taboo Category

Decadent Erotica is an anthology to please your deepest desires. It's a book of ten erotic stories to quench your fantasies and will also satisfy, intrigue, and enflame your passion. This sexy book includes stories about a pleasure Dom with his sub where he's addicted to making her climax, a couple who succumbs to dark alley impromptu intimacy, naughty office oral fun between coworkers, sneaky and intense nighttime passion between a husband and wife, and a scorching hot coffee shop that pushes all the limits. Not only will those steamy tales light up your yummy alone reading time, but so will the short stories about taboo female domination, a morning filled with surprise skin-on-skin rubs, but also thong panties plucked from the kitchen cabinet as inspiration for intimate relations, and a threesome rendezvous in a dressing room where female-female-male means extreme pleasure taken while in semi-public. And last but not by any means least, excite yourself with an extremely hot orgy party story.

Get this compilation of steamy spicy short stories from Ruan Willow all in one book. She's an erotica author, podcaster at Oh F*ck Yeah with Ruan Willow, sex blogger & influencer, and NSFW audiobook narrator. Some of these stories are also narrated by Ruan on the podcast. Check out her podcast which is free on podcast apps and on this site as well.

In audiobook with male narrators InMyHandsAudio, Your Nightly Desires, & Motorboatin' Matt https://books.ruanwillowauthor.com/decadenteroticaaudiobook

10 Tales of Extreme Sensuality, Indulgence, Dominance, and Submission (in ebook & paperback) https://books.ruanwillowauthor.com/decadenterotica

Anthologies and Award Nominations

Ruan has stories in the following anthologies:

He Will Obey (which was AWARDED THE 2020 SILVER PIGTAIL IN BEST ANTHOLOGY CATEGORY

The Femdom Coven (nominee for 2021 Golden Pigtail Smut Awards)

Inside of Ruan Willow (also available in an audiobook)

(this audiobook was a nominee for the 2021 Golden Pigtail Smut Awards)

https://books.ruanwillowauthor.com/insideofruanwillow

Decadent Erotica An Anthology **3rd Place Winner in the 2022 Golden Pigtails Smut Awards for Dark/Taboo Category**

https://books.ruanwillowauthor.com/decadenterotica

Other:

https://books.ruanwillowauthor.com/

Ruan's website with free erotic stories Ruan Willow Author[1]

Ruan's Patreon Ruan Willow on Patreon[2]

Ruan Willow on Goodreads Ruan Willow Goodreads Author page[3] Ruan Willow on BookBub https://www.bookbub.com/profile/ruan-willow

Sign up for Ruan's newsletter: https://subscribepage.io/ruanwillow

Subscribe to Ruan's Substack (Free and paid levels) https://ruanwillow.substack.com/

ARC copies are usually on BookSirens and StoryOrigin App. Check those sites for FREE ARC of books and audiobooks.

---

1. https://ruanwillowauthor.com/

2. https://www.patreon.com/ruanwillow

3. https://www.goodreads.com/author/show/21312130.Ruan_Willow

Made in the USA
Monee, IL
05 March 2025